POPPY

A Richard Jackson Book

POPPY

by AVI

illustrated by Brian Floca

ORCHARD BOOKS

NEW YORK

Fx: 2-00

For Cousin Amy

—A V I

Orchard Books, 95 Madison Avenue, New York, NY 10016

Manufactured in the United States of America
Book design by Mina Greenstein
The text of this book is set in 12 point Goudy Old Style.
The illustrations are pencil drawings reproduced in halftone.
10 9 8 7 6

Library of Congress Cataloging-in-Publication Data
Avi, date. Poppy / by Avi ; illustrated by Brian Floca.
p.   cm.   "A Richard Jackson book"—Half t.p.
Summary: Poppy the deer mouse urges her family to move
next to a field of corn big enough to feed them all forever,
but Mr. Ocax, a terrifying owl, has other ideas.
ISBN 0-531-09483-9   ISBN 0-531-08783-2 (lib. bdg.)
[1. Mice—Fiction. 2. Owls—Fiction. 3. Survival—
Fiction.] I. Floca, Brian, ill. II. Title.
PZ7.A953Po   1995   [Fic]—dc20   95-6040

CONTENTS

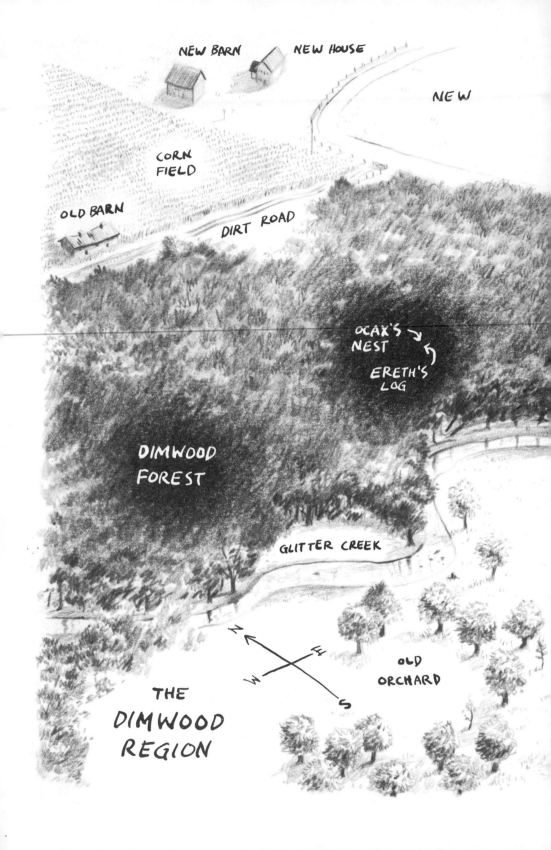

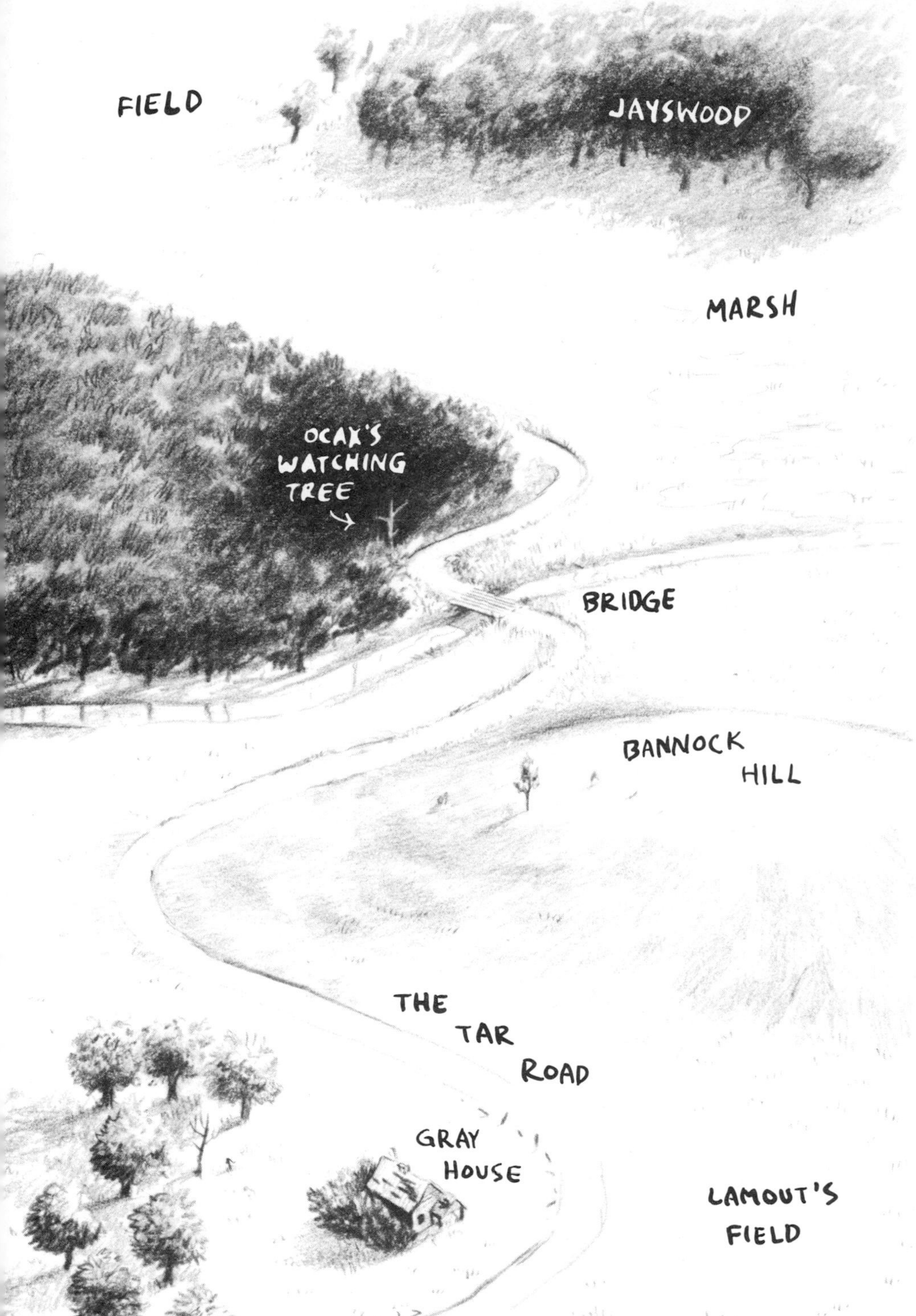

FIELD

JAYSWOOD

MARSH

OCAX'S
WATCHING
TREE

BRIDGE

BANNOCK
HILL

THE
TAR
ROAD

GRAY
HOUSE

LAMOUT'S
FIELD

I

Mr. Ocax

A thin crescent moon, high in the sky, shed faint white light over Dimwood Forest. Stars glowed. Breezes full of ripe summer fragrance floated over nearby meadow and hill. Dimwood itself, veiled in darkness, lay utterly still.

At the very edge of this forest stood an old charred oak on which sat a great horned owl. The owl's name was Mr. Ocax, and he looked like death himself.

Mr. Ocax's eyes—flat upon his face—were round and yellow with large ebony pupils that enabled him to see as few other creatures could. Moonlight—even faint moonlight— was as good as daylight for him.

With his piercing gaze, Mr. Ocax surveyed the lands he called his own, watching for the comings and goings of the creatures he considered his subjects—and his dinners. He looked at Glitter Creek, home to the fish he found so appetizing; the Tar Road, across which tasty rabbits were known to hop; Jayswood, where meaty chipmunks sometimes skittered before dawn. By swiveling his head he searched the Marsh for a savory frog, then New Field, where, usually, he could count on a delicious vole or two. He looked at Gray House, where Farmer Lamout used to live, then upon the Old Orchard. He even looked, nervously, toward New House. But nowhere did he see a thing to eat. Profoundly annoyed, Mr. Ocax was beginning to think he would have no dinner that night.

But finally, there—near the top of Bannock Hill, where the ponderosa pines had all been cut, where only a few struggling saplings and bushes grew—he saw movement. Just the glimmer of food was enough to cause his owl's heart to pound, his curved black beak to clack, his feathered horns to stand up tall.

Mr. Ocax shifted his head from right to left, forward and back. When he did so, he beheld . . . two mice! Of all the creatures the owl hunted, he enjoyed mice the most. They were the best eating, to be sure, but better still, they were the most fearful, and Mr. Ocax found deep satisfaction in having others afraid of him. And here, after a wait of nearly the whole night, were two savory subjects to terrify before he ate them.

One of the two, a deer mouse, crouched cautiously beneath a length of rotten bark. The other, a golden mouse, stood in the open on his hind legs, his short tail sticking straight out behind for balance. From his left ear an earring dangled. In his paws he held a hazelnut.

"It's not as if I haven't warned these mice," Mr. Ocax murmured to himself. "If they will move about without my permission, they have only themselves to blame for the consequences." As he leaned forward to listen, his sharp-as-needles talons, four to each large claw and jet-black at their tips, cut deeply into the branch he was perched on. "Catching these two mice," he mused, "is going to be fun."

On Bannock Hill, the golden mouse turned to his timid companion and said, "Poppy, girl, this hazelnut is bad-to-the-bone. Bet you seed to sap there's more where it came from. Come on out and dig."

"Ragweed," Poppy replied as she sniffed tensely in all directions, "you promised we'd dance when we got here. We can't do it in the open. Besides, I want to answer your question. So will you *please* get under here with me."

Ragweed laughed. "Dude, you must think I'm as dull as a dormouse. You just want to get some of this nut."

"I don't want any of your precious nut," Poppy insisted. "I want to give you my answer. And I want to dance! Isn't that the reason we came up the hill? Only it's not safe out there."

"Oh, tell me about it."

"You heard my father's warnings," Poppy went on. "It's Mr. Ocax. He might be watching and listening."

"Get off," Ragweed sneered. "Your pop talks about that Ocax dude just to scare you and keep you under control."

"Ragweed," Poppy cried, "that's ridiculous. Mr. Ocax *does* rule Dimwood. So we *have* to ask his permission to be here. And you know perfectly well we never did."

"Dude, I'm not going to spend my life asking an old owl's okay every time I want to have fun. Know what I'm saying? This is our moment, girl, right? And now that I've dug this nut up, I'm going to enjoy it. Besides," he said, "it's too dark for an old owl to see me."

"*Poppy,*" Mr. Ocax scoffed under his breath. "*Ragweed.* What stupid names mice have. Now, if only that deer mouse will move just a little farther out from under cover, I'll be able to snare *both* mice at once."

The mere thought of such a double catch made Mr. Ocax hiss with pleasure. Then he clacked his beak, spread his wings, and rose into the night air. Up he circled, his fluted flight feathers beating the air silently.

High above Bannock Hill, he looked down. The golden mouse—the one eating the nut—was still in the open. So brazen. So foolish. Nevertheless, Mr. Ocax decided to hold back another moment to see if the deer mouse might budge.

"Ragweed," Poppy pleaded, "please get under here."

"Girl," Ragweed said, "do you know what your problem is? You let your tail lead the way."

Poppy, hurt and wanting to show she was *not* a coward, poked her nose and whiskers out from under the bark. "Ragweed," she persisted even as she began to creep into the open, "being careless is stupid."

Her friend took another scrape of the nut and sighed with pleasure. "Poppy," he said, "you may be my best girl, but admit it, you don't know how to live like I do."

Poppy took two more steps beyond the bark.

Just then, Mr. Ocax pulled his wings close to his body and plunged. In an instant he was right above and behind the two mice. Once there, he threw out his wings—to brake his speed; pulled back his head—to protect his eyes; and

thrust his claws forward and wide like grappling hooks—to pounce.

It was Poppy who saw him. "Ragweed!" she shrieked in terror as she hurled herself back undercover. "It's Ocax!"

But the owl was already upon them. Down came his right claw. It scratched the tip of Poppy's nose. Down came his left claw. It was more successful, clamping around Ragweed's head and neck like a vise of needles, killing him instantly. The next moment the owl soared back into the air. A lifeless Ragweed—earring glittering in the moonlight—hung from a claw. As for the hazelnut, it fell to the earth like a cold stone.

Powerful but leisurely strokes brought Mr. Ocax back to his watching tree. Once there, he shifted the dead Ragweed from talon to beak in one gulp. The mouse disappeared down his throat, earring and all.

His hunger momentarily satisfied, Mr. Ocax tilted back his head and let forth a long, low cry of triumph. "Whooo-whooo!"

Poppy did not hear the call. In her terror she had fainted. Now she lay unconscious beneath the length of rotten bark.

The owl did not mind. He had enjoyed the first mouse so much he decided to wait for the second. Indeed, Mr. Ocax was not entirely sorry that Poppy had escaped. She was terrified, and he enjoyed that. And for sure, he would get her soon. "Oh yes," he murmured to himself, "mice *are* the most fun to catch." Then Mr. Ocax did that rare thing for an owl: He smiled.

2
Poppy Remembers

A stinging sensation on her nose woke Poppy. She touched a paw to the sore spot and winced. Then she looked about in the dark and shook her head with confusion. Where was she? Under a piece of rotten bark. Where was the bark? On Bannock Hill. What was she doing there? She had come with her boyfriend, Ragweed. Where was Ragweed?

No sooner did Poppy ask herself *that* than the full horror of what had occurred rushed upon her. Ragweed dead! Eaten, probably. Poppy closed her eyes. The sheer ghastliness of the thought made it hard for her to breathe.

Then, recalling how close *she* had come to the same fate, she checked herself for other injuries.

Though her plump, round belly was white, the rest of her fur was orange-brown. She had large ears and dark, almost round eyes, full whiskers, tiny nose, pink toes and tail. Even for a deer mouse, Poppy was rather dainty. Upon examination, everything—except the nose—seemed to be intact.

She stole a look out from under the bark and considered her situation. She was on Bannock Hill alone and without permission. Oh, how she wished she were home.

From her earliest days—just a few full moons ago—her parents had been teaching their litter about Mr. Ocax. She recalled how they had lined up all twelve of them to take instruction.

"Mr. Ocax has been about for ages," her father, Lungwort, lectured in his sternest voice. He was a rather stout fellow with elegantly curled whiskers and slightly protruding front teeth. His crowning glory was an ivory thimble he had found and which, ever since, he'd worn as a cap. "Mr. Ocax's been here longer than any mouse's living memory," Lungwort continued. "The territory around Dimwood *belongs* to him. Mr. Ocax is king."

"And he protects us," said Sweet Cicely, Lungwort's wife and Poppy's mother. "That's the most important thing." Sweet Cicely was a small creature even for a deer mouse, with soft, pale eyes and a nervous habit of flicking at her ears with her paws as if they were dusty.

"Protects us from what?" Poppy remembered Ragweed asking. An outsider, he had taken to hanging around the family. He was *always* asking for answers: "Why do deer mice live here and not there?" "Why do you folks eat this and not that?" "Why is your fur dark on top and white on bottom when mine is golden? Why couldn't it be the other way around?"

Though these constant questions could be irritating, Poppy had to admit that she'd often wondered about the answers. Curiosity, however, was not something her parents encouraged. Poppy admired Ragweed's persistence.

"Mr. Ocax protects us from creatures that eat us," Lungwort answered gravely. "Raccoons, foxes, skunks, weasels, stoats . . ." One by one he displayed pictures of these animals. "Most important, he protects us from *porcupines*. Like this one." He held up a lurid portrait of a huge black-nosed beast covered with gruesome spikes. Blood seemed to drip from his snarling mouth.

The young mice gasped in dread.

"Porcupines are our *particular* enemies," Lungwort insisted. "There is nothing porcupines won't do to catch mice."

"What would they do with us then?" Acorn, one of Poppy's sisters, asked in a trembling voice.

"First they shoot their barbed quills into you," Lungwort said.

"Then they trample you," Sweet Cicely added.

"Finally," Lungwort concluded, "they break you into little bits and gobble you up."

Now it was terror the young mice felt. All except Ragweed.

"Lungwort," he demanded, "other than that picture, *you* ever seen a porcupine? A *real* one?"

"Not precisely," Lungwort snapped. "But let me tell you something, Ragweed. I'd be more than thrilled to get through my whole life *without ever* seeing one. After all, Mr. Ocax has *seen* porcupines. Often. In private conversations with me—mind, these are actual personal experiences I can verify—he informed me that porcupines are not only extremely dangerous but also devilishly sly.

"Take note that this judgment comes from a powerful, meat-eating bird. The point is, Mr. Ocax protects us from porcupines. It was he, in fact, who was kind enough to educate us about them as well as supply these pictures."

"Then how come you have to worry about this dude Ocax, too?" Ragweed pressed.

Struggling to control his temper, Lungwort tapped his thimble cap down over his forehead. Fuming, he replied, "Mr. Ocax protects us from vicious porcupines only when we accept him as our ruler, that's why. All he requires is that we ask his permission whenever we move beyond the immediate area of Gray House.

"We have freedom to go about the Old Orchard up to Glitter Creek. We can do the same for Farmer Lamout's fields. At our own risk, of course. Life is full of danger. Go beyond, however, and we need to get Mr. Ocax's permission."

"What's his *reason*?" Ragweed persevered.

Sweet Cicely, brushing her ears, sighed with exasperation. How Poppy, her own daughter, could take up with such an ill-mannered ruffian was beyond her understanding. All the same, she said, "Ragweed, as Mr. Ocax has patiently explained to my husband, he needs to know if we're moving about so he won't mistake us for porcupines. Asking permission is a small sacrifice to pay for our safety."

Lungwort nodded his agreement. "That owl," he pointed out, "has incredible vision. *And* hearing. He can hear or see *anything*, even in the dark. And a good thing, too. Porcupines prowl at night. Move like lightning, Mr. Ocax says. Shoot quills without asking questions. Kill without mercy.

"No, my boy, we don't argue with Mr. Ocax. He's our

protector. If we disobey him, break his rules—and I can't say I blame him either—he gets upset."

"What'll he do then?" asked Leaf, one of Poppy's brothers.

"He'll eat you," Lungwort replied briskly as he put away the picture of the porcupine. "And," he continued, "it happens. During the past year we have lost some fifteen family members. It may be presumed that all failed to ask Mr. Ocax for permission to go somewhere."

The children were shocked into silence.

Ragweed, however, spoke out again. "Hey, Pops, didn't I hear you say porcupines are *huge?*"

"You saw the picture," Lungwort responded. "And don't call me Pops. It's common."

"So them porcupines are bigger than us, right?"

"A *lot* bigger," Sweet Cicely said, emphasizing the *lot*.

"Well, old lady," Ragweed kept on, "if them there porcupines are so huge, and we're so small, and if this dude owl has such amazing sight, how come he might confuse us mice with them there dude porcupines? Know what I'm saying?"

An indignant Sweet Cicely looked to her husband.

Lungwort sputtered, "Ragweed, for your information, proper grammatical usage is 'those porcupines,' not 'them there porcupines.' And while I'm thinking about it, if you intend to court my daughter I'll thank you to groom your hair properly when you get up in the morning. As for that earring you've taken to wearing, I don't like it. Not one bit. This family is committed to keeping up mice values and is *opposed* to stupid questions." With that, Lungwort stalked away, tail whipping about in agitation.

O*N BANNOCK HILL,* Poppy remembered it all. She also remembered it was Ragweed who insisted they come up the hill but that he absolutely refused to ask Mr. Ocax's permission to do so. Perhaps, then, what occurred—horrible as it had been—had served Ragweed right. Then and there Poppy vowed she would never leave home again.

The difficulty was that at that moment she was far from home, frightened, and alone.

3
Poppy Alone

Poppy glanced to the east. The horizon was streaked with layers of pink and red. Did that make it night or day? Neither. It was impossible to guess, then, if the owl was still awake, as he was at night, or asleep, as he was by day. Besides, the place in Dimwood Forest where Mr. Ocax slept—not the same as his watching post—was unknown. He kept it secret.

As if she might discover it, Poppy gazed into the forest. All she could make out was a great mass of dark trees. No wonder it was called *dim*, she thought, and shuddered.

Poppy considered the distance from the north side of Bannock Hill, where she was hiding, to the dwelling on the abandoned farm where she and her family lived—Gray House. It was about the length of four cornfields. Poppy decided she'd best race from one protected spot to another in quick, low belly runs.

She peeked out from beneath the bark again. There was a fallen branch up ahead, but it was leafless, so it would provide no cover. Beyond the branch, however, she spied a rock with a crevice just large enough to wedge into. Poppy decided to aim for that.

Whiskers stiffly alert, breathing deeply to catch the smallest whiff of danger, she crept out from under the protective piece of bark. If only, if only—she kept saying to herself—if only Mr. Ocax was not watching . . .

B*UT M*R*. O*CAX *was* watching. He was perched perfectly still on the dead branch of his tree, with very wide-open eyes. Not for a moment had he ceased staring at Poppy's hiding place. If there was one thing the owl hated more than a creature who neglected to ask permission to move about the territory, it was a creature who escaped punishment for *not* asking. How could he keep the mice terrified if any one of them got away with that? No, this Poppy must not escape!

Mr. Ocax belched, bringing up a pellet of Ragweed's bones and fur as well as the earring, which he had been unable to digest. The pellet fell to the ground to lie among a large pile of other pellets.

Intently, the owl moved his head from side to side, back and forth, adjusting his depth of vision. In time he saw Poppy's pink nose poke out from her hiding place. Then he watched as she raced toward a rock. At last! The mouse was on the move. Mr. Ocax clacked his beak with pleasure, spread his wings, and leaped into the air.

*P*ANTING hard but protected by the crevice, Poppy squirmed about and sniffed for hints of danger. She found none.

Once she had caught her breath, she edged a bit out of her nook and studied the terrain. The nearest haven she could see was a bush whose partly exposed roots straddled a hole big enough to shelter her. Unfortunately, the bush was on the far side of a flat, open space, a long way from where she crouched. It was farther, by far, than the length of Gray House's attic; farther even than the water pump beyond the back door; farther, in fact, than Poppy had ever run without stopping to rest. She sighed with dismay.

Then she looked again. This time she spied a rectangular strip of wood propped against a stone at an upward angle. It was about halfway between where she hunched and the hole. Poppy told herself that if she tired, or if some danger appeared, she would be able to hide—briefly—beneath the high end.

Tense, she examined the eastern sky once more. It had grown lighter. Was it day yet? Would Mr. Ocax be asleep *now*?

*T*HE OWL, cruising high to the west of Bannock Hill, moved his wings slowly, wanting to make the least possible disturbance on the air. These deer mice, he knew, could be very sensitive.

As he flew, he kept his eyes fixed on Poppy's rock. The mouse's run suggested what she was doing, moving from protected spot to protected spot. Mr. Ocax was well aware that the biggest family of deer mice in his territory—headed by that old fool Lungwort—lived in Gray House. More than likely this Poppy was heading there. Well, then, how would she go?

The owl spied a bush on the south side of the hill. Though it was some distance from the rock, it would be a logical next hiding place for the mouse. But if it came to a race for that bush, he knew who would win. Mr. Ocax gave a hiss of satisfaction.

*P*OPPY cleared the rock crevice in one jump. Her landing, however, was awkward. It threw up a puff of dust. Swiftly she scrambled back to her feet, then started to dash across the open area. Belly low, tail stiff as a nail, ears folded back, she pumped her legs like pistons.

MR. OCAX, circling above, saw the dust caused by the mouse's jump. The next moment he spotted Poppy. In a flash he calculated her speed and direction. Determining the exact spot where he could catch her, he made four quick, strong wing pumps, which brought him to the proper altitude. Then he dived.

POPPY streaked over the ground. Though she felt as though her heart would burst, she was almost halfway to the bush. Soon she would be passing the wood strip.

MR. OCAX, who had plummeted to a spot not far above and behind Poppy, threw out his wings, pulled back his head, thrust his claws forward. In anticipation of the meal he was about to eat, he clacked his beak.

POPPY, hearing the clack, cast a lightning glance over her shoulder. Mr. Ocax was right behind her, his fearsome talons set. The shock of seeing the owl so close surged through her like a bolt of electricity. With an enormous kick of her rear legs she shot into the air, tumbling head over heels until she came down, belly flat, on the far end of the length of wood.

POPPY's leap caught Mr. Ocax by surprise. As he dived, Poppy took off. Sensing he would miss her, he adjusted. Up came his claws. Down went his left wing. Over went his tail. What Mr. Ocax achieved, however, was a careening swerve that brought him crashing beyond his target, onto the same strip of wood as Poppy—but on the *opposite* end.

When Mr. Ocax landed, his weight catapulted the light-as-a-feather mouse into the air in a great arc that dumped her with a splat right at the base of the bush. Frantic, she clawed forward and tumbled head over heels into the hole she'd been aiming for.

MR. OCAX swiveled his head first this way, then that, searching for his prey. She seemed to have vanished.

Frustrated, he flapped into the air and circled low over Bannock Hill but found no trace. Seething, the owl headed back to Dimwood. How dare this mouse—this Poppy—escape! Twice! Never before had a mouse done that. Mr.

Ocax had half a mind to return
to his watching tree and wait for the
impudent creature to pop up. The next
moment he decided against it. He was tired.
Daylight had finally arrived. It was long past
his sleeping time. Besides, he had eaten something.

But as Mr. Ocax sailed deep into Dimwood toward his
secret lair, he vowed to avenge himself. If mice began to
get notions that they could escape him, there would be no
end of trouble.

Poppy lay in the hole beneath the bush, hurting from
ears to tail. It took time for her breathing to become regular,
longer still for her pulse to drop to normal.

When she began to feel herself again, she tested her
legs and toes to see if they worked. Everything seemed to
be intact. Cautiously she crawled to the top of the hole
and stole a quick peek. Though she saw no sign of Mr.
Ocax, she retreated hastily, still too agitated to do anything
but hide.

It was some time before Poppy took another look. Then
she took a third. Though she still didn't see the owl, she
hesitated. Mr. Ocax, she knew, was capable of great patience.

So it was that the sun had risen quite high above the
horizon before Poppy finally eased herself out of the hole.
Following her plan of short runs and safe havens, she scampered at last down Bannock Hill to Gray House.

According to mice family stories, a human called Farmer Lamout had lived in the house. When he and his family left—it was said to be many, many winters ago—the house started to collapse. The white walls turned ashen. The roof's middle dropped lower than either end. Windows fell out. Doors fell in. The farmer's cast-off boots, old furniture, magazines crumbled. All in all, it was a perfect and safe home for Poppy's family.

But as Poppy approached the house, she spied a small red flag hanging from one end of the roof. She stopped short. A red flag was her father's signal that the entire clan needed to gather for an emergency meeting.

Poppy's first thought was that news of Ragweed's death had already reached home. Then she realized how unlikely that was. Something else of grave importance must have occurred.

4
The Emergency Meeting

Poppy ran across the lopsided porch and into the parlor. The whole family had indeed gathered. Poppy's father, thimble on his head, was on his accustomed perch atop an old straw hat, already addressing the crowd. The moment Poppy entered the room, he saw her.

"Ah, Poppy," he cried, "you're late, but at least you're here."

All the mice—a sea of ears, eyes, pink noses, and whiskers—turned to look at her.

"But where's Ragweed?" Lungwort demanded. "Wasn't he with you? Do you think he'll have the common decency, not to mention courtesy, to consider joining us at this moment of crisis? Or is he beyond all that?"

With so many eyes fixed on her, Poppy could not speak.

"Well, Poppy?" Lungwort asked. "*Do* you know where your friend is?"

Poppy stammered, "May I tell you after the meeting?"

Lungwort murmured a "Humph," as well as an "I suppose," and "Thoughtless children," concluding with, "Just take your place, please."

Poppy slipped forward and crouched down next to Basil, her favorite younger cousin.

"Where you guys been?" Basil whispered.

"Out," Poppy replied weakly.

"You don't look so good. What happened to your nose?"

"I can't explain now."

"And where *is* Ragweed?"

"Later," Poppy insisted.

Basil gave his cousin a questioning look but held his tongue.

Lungwort, leaning over the crown of the farmer's hat, tapped his thimble cap and held up a paw to command silence. "For Poppy's sake," he began, "I'll review what I've said already. Our family has grown very large. So large, in fact, that there is not enough food in this neighborhood to feed us all.

"Indeed, our family is still an expanding one." He nodded to Sweet Cicely, who smiled wanly in dutiful recognition of the remark. "For example," Lungwort continued, "my wife and I have had seventy-five children, who in turn have given us forty grandchildren, twenty great-grandchildren, and twelve great-great-grandchildren."

This remark was greeted by the assembled mice with a generous tapping of tails upon the floor.

Lungwort dipped his head in acknowledgment of the tribute. Then he went on. "The truth is, by my calculations, our current rate of population growth—and it's this I was about to say when Poppy arrived—promises serious food shortages, sickness, and, yes, death, unless we take action within the next few days."

There was an immediate buzz and squeak among the family. "Good grief!" "How awful!" "What'll we do now?" "Who would have guessed?"

Lungwort raised his voice over the hubbub. "Living in the open will not do. The dangers of that are obvious. No, we need to establish an extra residence—a home near to abundant food but still close enough to Gray House so that the family, with its present leadership, can be maintained. And of course, the second dwelling must be safe.

"Happily, I have been informed by an old sparrow acquaintance of mine—Mr. Albicollis—that a new home has been built within the territory."

Again there was chatter. "Where?" "Have you seen it?" "What's it like?"

"It's on the northern side of Dimwood Forest. New House, it's called. A half day's trek from here."

"That's so far!" "Almost another country!" "I've never been away from home!" "I bet it's not so good as this place!"

Lungwort held up a paw. The talk stilled. "This New House is reachable by the Tar Road, across the Bridge, and beyond New Field, which, I've been informed, has abundant food."

"Somebody else can go!" "Wonder what kind of food there is." "I doubt I'd do well there!"

"Naturally, I will need to investigate New House with care."

"Would I get a room of my own?" "Can I keep sharing with Tansy?" "They'll never get me to go." "I won't bunk with Husk."

"Further, there will be much organizing and packing to be done."

"I hate the thought of packing." "I have too much to move." "I just put together a whole new room."

"Finally," Lungwort went on, "we will need a delegation to go through the formality of applying to Mr. Ocax for permission to move."

This time Lungwort's words brought silence. Every eye looked down or away. Except for Poppy's. She could only stare at her father in revulsion. How could he even suggest such a thing!

"Now, now," Lungwort said severely, "Mr. Ocax has always been most accommodating. Need I remind you that he protects us from porcupines. We all know about porcupines, don't we? We do indeed. Have we seen so much as *one* porcupine in these parts for years? Not one! Proof enough that Mr. Ocax is holding up *his* end of the bargain. As long as I'm head of this family, I expect us to do *our* part. Asking his permission to move is an insignificant sacrifice to make for our well-being.

"All right, then," Lungwort concluded, looking around. "Any questions?"

Poppy had no idea what Ragweed would have asked,
but she knew it would have been *something*.

"Good," Lungwort said. "I thank you for your attention.
Go about your business. I will keep you informed as always.
Poppy, be so good as to remain. I'd like a private word."

With much excited chatter the mice scurried off until
only Poppy, her parents, and Basil remained.

"*Now* can you tell me what's going on?" Basil asked.
"You're really looking bad."

Poppy, trying to find the words to tell her parents about Ragweed, had closed her eyes.

Basil tugged at her. "Poppy, did something happen to Ragweed?"

Poppy gave a quick nod.

"What?"

"Poppy!" her father called from across the parlor. "I'm waiting!"

Poppy opened her eyes and turned to Basil. "Stay close," she said to him. "I'm going to need you."

Slowly Poppy crept toward her parents. Basil trailed behind.

As his daughter approached, Lungwort drew himself up with a show of dignity. "Well, Poppy," he said, "I suppose I should be grateful that you managed to find time for a family meeting."

"Papa," Poppy began, "you see . . ."

Suddenly Sweet Cicely asked, "Poppy, what did you do to your nose?"

"It's that—"

"We can deal with her nose later," Lungwort interrupted. "What I wish to say first, Poppy, is this: As I made my announcement about the house—you did hear it, didn't you?"

"Yes."

"When I mentioned making up a delegation to go to Mr. Ocax, I was saddened that not one of your brethren or sistern would look me in the eye. It was as if they were fearful. But you, Poppy, were steady on the mark. Your eye never wavered. Straight and loyal. I admire that in a young mouse.

"Therefore I have selected you, by way of a reward— and it is a grand one, isn't it, Mother?"

Sweet Cicely, brushing at her ears, smiled thinly.

"Right, then," Lungwort continued. "Poppy, I have selected *you* to go with me to Mr. Ocax."

"You *what?*" Poppy cried.

"I know it's an unlooked-for honor. But you heard me right. You will join me when I go to Mr. Ocax."

"But . . . but . . . ." Poppy tried to find words but could not.

"But what?"

"But Mr. Ocax just *ate* Ragweed!" Poppy blurted out.

There was stunned silence.

"*Ate Ragweed?*" Sweet Cicely finally gasped, her voice half gargle, half squeak. "Did I hear you correctly?"

Trying to stop her tears, Poppy nodded.

"When?" Lungwort demanded shrilly. "How? Why didn't you tell me?"

"I barely got back," Poppy sobbed. "And when I walked into the meeting, I couldn't just say . . ." Pawing the tears from her face, she whispered, "I *couldn't.*"

"But to be eaten by Mr. Ocax," Lungwort sputtered, "without even informing me . . . !"

Sweet Cicely suddenly turned on her husband. "Oh, stop that!" she cried. "We need to know what happened. Poppy, go on."

Poppy, her heart heavy, stammered, "We, that is, Ragweed and I . . . last night we went out to Bannock Hill. I mean, we had never been before. It was such a beautiful summer night, and we thought it would be romantic. It *was* lovely. And he had just asked me . . ." Poppy paused to look at her parents. Certain they would not be sympathetic, she decided to skip some parts of her story.

"Then Ragweed found a hazelnut," she went on. "He loves—loved—nuts. So he started to eat it. I told him that he should get under cover. He wouldn't listen. And then—all of a sudden—out of *nowhere*—Mr. Ocax burst upon us. I hadn't heard a thing. He was just *there*. He almost got me, too," she added, pointing to her nose. "But he caught Ragweed," she whispered. "It was awful."

Sweet Cicely hurried forward, gathered her daughter in a hug, and patted her back. A very uncomfortable Lungwort kept clearing his throat and fiddling with his whiskers.

"And then," Poppy went on once she was sufficiently calmed, "when I started back home, Mr. Ocax tried to catch me—*again*. But I managed to escape."

Lungwort shook his head. "Poppy," he intoned, "I'm bound to ask: Did you go through the proper formalities before going up on the hill?"

"Well, I, that is, we . . ."

"Come now!" Lungwort cried, his agitation bursting out as anger. "Did you or did you not ask Mr. Ocax for permission to go up there? Answer me!"

"No," Poppy admitted.

"Well, then," Lungwort said, "if Ragweed's death can be an object lesson to the rest of the family, perhaps what happened will serve a useful purpose. Good out of bad, so to speak."

"Ragweed wasn't bad," Poppy objected.

"I never said he was bad. But without doubt his *thinking* was bad. He was a rude, thoughtless, headstrong mouse. Not one of ours, may I point out. Indeed, if your friend had followed rules, if he had accepted things as they are, if he had listened to *me*, he would be with us today."

"Such a short, unhappy life." Sweet Cicely sighed.

"I warned him, Poppy," Lungwort declared. "I did. Let no mouse say otherwise. Though he was no son of mine, I did my duty by him, but he would not pay heed. There should be a lesson learned from this."

Poppy tried to protest. "But Ragweed and I—"

Again Lungwort interrupted. "Poppy, two things. First,

I want you to go among the rest of the family and explain what happened to your unfortunate friend. Be so kind as to point out the cause: that you did *not* ask permission from Mr. Ocax. I desire no such tragedies to befall one of *us*. Is that understood?"

"Yes, sir."

"Second, what I said stands about your coming with me when I request permission from Mr. Ocax for our move. Let's hope your presence will convince him that, one, you truly are apologetic for what you have done, and two, in the future you will ask for his permission before venturing anywhere."

So saying, Lungwort, with one paw about Sweet Cicely, went off, leaving Poppy and Basil alone.

Poppy looked after them for such a long time that Basil reached out and touched her. "Poppy?" he asked. "You all right?"

"Basil," Poppy said with a mix of sadness and anger, "Ragweed *wasn't* unhappy or bad. He *wasn't*. Maybe he was cocky at times—but I loved him for it. I did!" Once again tears trickled down her face.

"Poppy," Basil asked, "are you really going to go to Mr. Ocax?"

"I don't think I have much choice, do I? Only I do wonder what'll happen when he recognizes me."

Her cousin's eyes grew wide. "Think he will?"

Poppy pointed to the scratch on her nose. "How can he miss? He put this there."

5
Leaving Gray House

For the next two days Lungwort worked on the speech he intended to make to Mr. Ocax. He did this in his study, an old boot that Farmer Lamout had left behind the front hall steps. After lining the boot with potato sacking, Lungwort had chewed out a couple of windows, then used a plaid necktie to curtain the entryway.

Now and again he emerged, papers in hand. Seeking out older members of the family, he'd corner them and say, "I need you to listen to this."

After reading a paragraph or two, he insisted upon knowing what the listener thought. If there were compliments, he said something like, "No, I don't want flattery. I can't use that. I need hard criticism." When he received criticism, he always argued that his way was best. Then off he'd go—in a grump—to make minute subtractions or additions to his text, none of which had anything to do with either compliments *or* criticisms.

While Lungwort prepared his speech, a committee busied itself making a white flag. No one knew whether a flag of this kind was Lungwort's idea or Mr. Ocax's demand. Even so, whenever there was such a "permission party," as the younger mice called it, a crisp new flag was carried so Mr. Ocax would have no doubt as to the mice's intentions. It would be Poppy's job to march along with her father, bearing the flag.

Poppy, meanwhile, did what she'd been told to do, relating the facts of Ragweed's death to all the family. Everyone was upset by the story. Being eaten by Mr. Ocax was a shared nightmare. Moreover, it happened with some regularity. They were all scared of him. There was considerable "Tut-tutting," and much whisker twitching. Yet, while everyone expressed sorrow, Poppy suspected that few grieved. Worst were the words of comfort that began, "Well, if someone had to be sacrificed . . ."

"I don't understand why they disliked Ragweed so," Poppy protested sadly to Basil the night before she and Lungwort were to go see Mr. Ocax. "What harm did Ragweed do them?"

"I can think of three things," Basil replied. "He was a golden mouse, not a deer mouse. He came from somewhere else. And he said things that upset them. You know, like, 'You haven't lived unless you die for something.' Remember what he told old Plum? 'A soft belly causes softness at both ends.' "

"But I liked that he was different," Poppy confessed. "He loved adventure. I'll never forget the last words he ever spoke to me. They were so terribly ironic."

"What's *ironic?*"

"You know, when the words mean almost the opposite of what you're saying. The last thing he said to me was 'You don't know how to live like I do.' "

"What's ironic about that?" Basil asked.

"The next second Mr. Ocax killed him."

"Oh!" Basil shuddered.

"Now, Poppy," her mother began as she brushed her daughter's fur for a final time, "above all, do *exactly* what your father tells you to do.

"Be respectful toward Mr. Ocax if he takes notice of you. But if he does not, don't fret. Your father commands his attention. Mr. Ocax has great respect for your father.

"Don't so much as squeak until you are spoken to. Then be humble and brief.

"Remember the old saying 'Mice should be nice.' And for heaven's sake, keep the white flag flying.

"Above all," Sweet Cicely concluded, "remember, it's an honor that you were selected to go."

"Yes, Mother," Poppy replied, though what her mother was saying made her very uncomfortable.

Lungwort appeared at that moment. His hair was slicked down; his whiskers were crisply curled; his tail had been scrubbed to a glowing pink; his thimble hat was set at a natty angle. "Is she ready?" he asked his wife.

"I think so."

Lungwort examined his daughter with a critical eye. "Fine," he said. "A good start promises a good finish. All right, Mother, we should be off."

Sweet Cicely gave Lungwort a nuzzle, whispering, "Do be careful."

"Careful is my middle name," Lungwort assured her, and led the way to the porch. There the whole family of mice had assembled for a send-off. Fireflies had been gathered and, now released, gave the moment a festive mood. Poppy, holding the flag, stood at the foot of the porch steps.

Lungwort scampered atop the old porch rail and faced the crowd.

"My fellow mice," he began, paws clasped comfortably over his plump belly while he surveyed his family with solemn regard, "I am about to leave for my meeting with Mr. Ocax. Need I remind you how important is this deputation? A moment for the multitude of mice to memorize."

Poppy, unable to make much sense of the words, stopped listening. She was searching for Basil in the crowd.

"Be certain," Lungwort continued, "that I will go forward with your best interests at heart. I have prepared a fine speech that will, I'm sure, convince him of our needs." He held up a scroll of paper, wrapped carefully in leaves to protect it. "I look forward to returning with Mr. Ocax's kind permission so at least half of us can move on to a new home. That will be a great day for us all."

At this point he looked down at Poppy. "Poppy," he cried, "raise up the flag!"

"What?"

"The flag, Poppy! The flag!"

"Oh!" Poppy lifted the white banner high. Looking at
it, all she could think of was a flag of surrender.

As Lungwort took his place before her, one of the crowd
called out, "Hip-hip—"

"Hurrah!" cried the others.

"Hip-hip—"

"Hurrah!"

"Forward!" Lungwort cried. He gave a smart nod to Poppy, and they began to march off. The crowd continued to cheer. Poppy had to admit it was grand. When she caught sight of Basil waving frantically to catch her eye, she even felt proud.

Within moments, however, everything changed. Gray House, with its cheerful lights and well-wishers, vanished behind them. The moon had all but disappeared behind clouds that promised rain. No stars were visible. The air felt as heavy as wet wool. In the darkness, Poppy had no idea of which direction they were to go.

"We'll be taking the Tar Road," Lungwort informed her. "Fewer obstructions. More visibility."

"Do we have a meeting place?" she asked.

"The very tip of Dimwood Forest," her father said. "Just on the far side of the Bridge over Glitter Creek. Mr. Ocax's watching tree. He's there most nights. Can't miss it. It's a huge dead oak."

"How come it's dead?"

"It was hit by lightning."

"Was Mr. Ocax on the tree at the time?"

Lungwort chuckled. "Poppy, there are those who say Mr. Ocax made the lightning himself. He's that kind of bird. Now, my dear, do keep that flag up."

Poppy tried, but she was wondering what kind of chance they'd have with an owl who made his own lightning.

Marching down the middle of the Road made her nervous. Surely Mr. Ocax would see them. Would he recognize her? If he did, would he attack? What should she do then? Run? Where? Ashamed to have such worries, Poppy decided it would be better to hide them. So she said nothing. Still, it was hard to keep the heavy flag high.

"Up!" Lungwort kept calling. He was now walking behind her.

They had been marching for some time—during which they had exchanged only a few words—when the night silence was suddenly shattered by a "Whooo-whooo!"

Startled, Poppy stopped short. In the confusion, Lungwort banged into her. He lost his thimble cap and his speech. She dropped the flag.

"Pick the flag up!" her father cried, searching and finding both thimble and speech in the darkness. "Lose the flag and we're done for!"

"Do you think he's seen us?"

"Why else do you think he called?" Lungwort snapped.

The hair along Poppy's spine stood straight up. It wasn't the owl's call that frightened her as much as the fear she heard suddenly in her father's voice. Never had she heard that before. She peered around at him. He didn't appear scared. Poppy sighed. She decided she must have imagined it, seeing in him what *she* was feeling.

The call came again: "Whooo-whooo."

Poppy, her heart pounding, asked, "How much farther to go?"

"Quite a ways," Lungwort whispered.

They listened again. No more calls came. Lungwort adjusted his hat and gave a forced chuckle. "Actually, I suspect that call was just some good-natured joshing."

"Papa?"

"What?"

"I'm glad you're here."

"Humph," Lungwort replied, but Poppy sensed he was pleased. She felt better until he said, "But do keep that flag up."

The owl's call came again. For a second time Poppy stopped. Her father did, too. They listened intently for a few moments. Then Lungwort whispered, "Just as I thought. He's joking. Lighten up, child." They moved on.

Poppy didn't like to contradict her father, but she doubted Mr. Ocax's calls were a joke. She rather suspected the owl was trying to scare them. And—as far as she was concerned—he was succeeding.

Rain began. It came softly at first, but when a clap of thunder burst right overhead—making them jump—the drizzle turned into a deluge. Within seconds they were soaked. The tar-covered road ran with water. The flag became heavier and spattered with mud.

"Shake out the flag," Lungwort cried. "It must stay white."

Poppy tried to do as she was told, but it was difficult.

They trudged on. Off to the left, flashes of lightning allowed Poppy to see the tall trees of Dimwood Forest. Although she, like all the mice, was well aware of the forest, she had never visited it. Who would want to? She'd been taught too many fearsome things about its vast size, its dreadful darkness, the fact that Mr. Ocax had a secret home there. Equally alarming was the knowledge that Dimwood Forest was full of the animals that hunted mice, animals like porcupines. Poppy made herself look in another direction.

"We're getting close," her father said, his voice tense.

Poppy cocked an ear. Over the continual splash of rain, she heard the rushing waters of Glitter Creek. Then the Tar Road twisted sharply to the left. They had reached the Bridge, a row of heavy wooden planks thrown across the creek. The gaps between the planks were wide enough for a mouse to fall through. Lungwort chose the middle plank and Poppy followed.

Despite her best intentions, she couldn't keep from peeking down. Normally Glitter Creek was serene. The summer rains had made it high, fast, and fairly roaring.

Poppy stole a nervous glance at her father. He had stopped to pull at his whiskers. She had never seen him so agitated and wondered suddenly if he would be able to protect her. She'd never asked the question before. Never had to. Just to think it upset her. She looked to her father for reassurance, but all she saw was his frailty. She *knew* then that he was just as frightened as she was. The realization made her stomach ache with tension.

Lungwort caught her looking at him. "Flag!" he cried, moving forward.

Poppy managed to lever the flag up just as she stepped off the Bridge. The moment she did, the air was rent with yet another of Mr. Ocax's cries: "Whooo-whooo!"

"There he is!" Lungwort exclaimed.

Poppy looked up. As the lightning flashed and thunder rumbled, Mr. Ocax's dead oak seemed to leap toward them. Against the darkness of Dimwood she saw that the owl's branch reached out like a claw. As for Mr. Ocax, his head feathers were erect, making him look like a devil.

"Don't give way!" Poppy said fiercely to herself even as she trembled. "Don't give way!"

6

Standing before Mr. Ocax

The leaves of the oak trees around Mr. Ocax's oak shielded him from the rain, but Poppy and her father were being drenched. The owl's head, moreover, was pulled down between his wings, while his eyes, enormously wide and unblinking, gave Poppy the sensation that there was nothing she might do or even *think* of doing which he could not, would not, see. To Poppy he seemed to be pure power and fury.

Wanting to look away, she glanced at the base of Mr. Ocax's tree. There lay what appeared to be a mound of pebbles. Gradually a ghastly realization came over her. What she was seeing was a mound of Mr. Ocax's upchucked pellets, the closely packed and undigested bits of fur and bone from his dinners. The vision made her blood turn cold. Only the sound of Mr. Ocax's sneering voice jolted her back to alertness.

"What do you want, Lungwort?" the owl demanded, his claws continually flexing on his perch.

Lungwort, holding cap in hand like an empty bucket, said, "May I wish you a very pleasant evening, Mr. Ocax?"

"It's not very pleasant," Mr. Ocax returned with a snarl.

"No, well, you're absolutely right there, Mr. Ocax," Lungwort replied, straining to sound jaunty. "But April showers, as the song goes, bring May flowers. And I—"

Mr. Ocax clacked his beak. "Lungwort, it's summer. Did you come here to sing me idiot songs, or do you have something important to say?"

"Well, in fact, I did bring—"

"Hurry up. I've not eaten my dinner yet. And I'm hungry."

"Well, yes, of course," Lungwort said. "I understand perfectly."

Lungwort hastily put on his hat, not noticing until too late that it had filled with rain. Water cascaded over his head. With a nervous shake, he fumbled to unroll his speech paper. Before he could get it out, Mr. Ocax's eyes grew bigger.

"Who's that?" he demanded as he moved his head about to bring Poppy into better focus.

"Forgive me," Lungwort said. "I've been rude. This is one of my dutiful daughters. Poppy, step forward. Look up. There's the good mouse. Mr. Ocax, may I introduce Poppy to you?"

Prodded by her father, she stepped forward gingerly. All

she could see was Mr. Ocax's eyes. She felt not just looked at but attacked.

"Poppy, eh?" he growled. "I think we've already met."

"One of my sweetest," Lungwort offered.

Mr. Ocax ignored him. Instead he said, "What happened to your nose, girl?"

"I . . . I . . . scraped it."

"A close call, I'd say."

"Yes, sir."

"Little girl mice should be more careful."

"Yes, sir."

"Do you understand me?"

Poppy longed to run away.

Lungwort nudged her. "Poppy, dear, Mr. Ocax asked if you were understanding him."

"Yes, sir, I do," Poppy squeaked with a bob of her head.

"All right, then," Mr. Ocax said. "Now be a good little girl and come stand under my tree while I talk to your father."

Hating herself for acting so fearful, queasy at the thought of going closer to the mound of pellets, Poppy appealed to her father with a look. Lungwort, however, only nodded.

"Move it!" Mr. Ocax snapped.

Averting her eyes from the pellets, Poppy crept toward the tree, the flag dragging behind her. But when she reached the spot, she was unable to resist the fascination of the horrible mound. Once she looked, she caught sight of something that glittered.

"All right, Lungwort," Mr. Ocax said, "let's hear what you have to say."

"Thank you, sir. Thank you." Lungwort held out his piece of paper. Now the thimbleful of water, as well as the rain, had drenched it. All the same, he tried to read:

"Whereas Mr. Ocax, Great Horned Owl, Ruler of the Dimwood Forest Region, who, out of his kindness and wisdom, protects all members of the Deer Mice family:

"Whereas the said family of Deer Mice living in Gray House, in return for Mr. Ocax's protection, have agreed to ask his permission whenever they wish to move about:

"Whereas the Deer Mice family, having grown so great in numbers, need a second place of habitation so as to maintain and enhance their lives with sufficient food:

"And . . ." Lungwort paused to shake the paper.

"And what?" Mr. Ocax demanded.

"The paper is somewhat wet," Lungwort apologized.

"So is the style," Mr. Ocax observed. "Go on."

Lungwort cleared his throat and continued to read. "Whereas Mr. Ocax, Protector of Deer Mice, is famous for his kindness, generosity, and compassion:

"Theref—"

"Stop!"

"Yes?"

"Repeat that!"

"What?"

"That line about me."

"About kindness, generosity, and compassion?"

"Right. I like it. *That's* well written."

"Yes, thank you. I wrote it. Whereas Mr. Ocax, Protector of Deer Mice, is famous for his kindness, generosity, and compassion:

"Therefore, said Deer Mice of said Gray House humbly petition said Mr. Ocax to . . . to . . ."

"Will you get to the point!" Mr. Ocax screeched in exasperation.

"I'm sorry," Lungwort said. "The rain has washed away the rest of my writing."

"Then just dump it and say what you want," the owl boomed.

"We . . . we humbly request your permission," Lungwort finally said, "to move."

"*Move?*"

"Yes."

"Why?"

"I said, we are too many. We need more food."

"Where do you want to go?"

"To New House."

First Mr. Ocax blinked. Next he swiveled his head around, frowning first at Lungwort, then down at Poppy, then again at Lungwort. Finally he said, "You mean that new place up along the Tar Road, beyond New Field?"

Poppy thought she heard something new in Mr. Ocax's voice. She tried to grasp it.

"Yes, sir."

Mr. Ocax hesitated. "Well . . . er . . . have you been there?"

Now Poppy was sure. It was *uncertainty* that she was hearing.

"*Have* you been there?" Mr. Ocax demanded shrilly.

"Well, the truth is," Lungwort said, "my friend Mr.—"

"*Yes or no?*" the owl screamed.

"Well, no. Not exactly. But my friend told me it would

make an excellent source of food for half of my family, and—"

"Lungwort!" Mr. Ocax interrupted. "I forbid you to move to New House."

"What?" Lungwort gasped, flapping the rain away from his face with a paw. The word had all but stuck in his throat.

"Permission *denied*, Lungwort. You cannot move to New House."

"But, but—why, sir?"

"Because I said so."

"But . . . but the Gray House area does not provide enough food. It's urgent that some of us move so we can survive and—"

"*No New House.* Now I've got a dinner to catch, so you'd better skedaddle. Unless, of course, you want to please me by leaving your daughter. Then"—the owl chuckled—"I might reconsider."

"But . . ."

Mr. Ocax leaned forward. "Whooo-whooo," he wailed in his loudest but lowest voice.

The sound exploded over them. Poppy, clapping paws to ears, ran out from under the tree toward her father, who was still standing there, stammering, "But . . . but . . ."

"Come on, Papa," Poppy urged, trying to turn her father around. "We'd better go." With difficulty she turned him.

"Lungwort!" Mr. Ocax called suddenly.

Lungwort whirled so fast the thimble fell off his head.

Bowing, smiling, he began, "You were just teasing, weren't—"

"Listen to me, Lungwort!" Mr. Ocax cried. "I've two more things to say to you. First! Pass the word among your friends that I've spotted a new porcupine around Dimwood."

"Porcupine?" Lungwort echoed dumbly.

"A particularly vicious one. But don't worry. I'll protect you. Second . . . it's about your daughter there. If you want a *reason* for my refusal, ask her how she and I met before."

"Reason?"

"She didn't ask permission to go to the hill. *That's* why you can't go to New House."

"Yes, but—"

"Beat it, Lungwort. Now!"

"Come on, Papa. We'd better leave."

Lungwort glanced about for his thimble hat. It had rolled away. It was Poppy who retrieved it and put it on his head. Resigned, a sagging Lungwort allowed himself to be led away. Poppy glanced at her father. All traces of dignity were gone. The wetness that ran down his face was not rain but tears.

Poppy hardly tried to keep the flag aloft. And as they trudged home, she kept stealing looks into one of her paws. In it was clenched something she had pried from one of Mr. Ocax's pellets: Ragweed's earring.

7
Home Again

Poppy and her father did not talk on the long way home. Only occasionally did she say, "Watch the puddle, Papa," or, "Won't be long now." That was all.

Lungwort, walking with his head down, eyes glued to his feet, kept uttering sighs. Now and then he reached up to touch his hat, just to be sure it was there. Once, after stealing a look at Poppy—a look that she caught—he let out something like a moan.

Poppy was fearful of asking her father the questions she kept asking herself: If Mr. Ocax refused permission for the move—and he had—and if there was not enough food—and her father said *that* was true—what was the family to do? Would some of them have to forage in distant places, in the open? That meant they'd be at the mercy of Mr. Ocax, a complete calamity.

Poppy peeked again at Ragweed's earring. She kept asking herself why had she ever gone to the hill with Ragweed without asking permission. She knew better. Look at all the trouble she'd caused. Just then she hated herself for having loved Ragweed. But just to think that thought made her heart ache.

Rain was still falling when they reached Gray House. Both mice were soaked and exhausted. The once white flag trailed in the mud.

A large number of mice were milling about on the porch waiting for the expected good news. Sure enough, when Poppy and Lungwort appeared, a cheer went up.

The sound brought Lungwort to a dead halt. The old mouse stared blankly at the rows of eager faces. A second cheer began but faded as the onlookers sensed something was wrong.

Silent and grim-faced, eyes averted, Lungwort painfully climbed the Gray House steps. Alarmed into silence, the mice backed away to let him pass.

Poppy saw her mother break through the crowd. "Lungwort!" she cried. "Oh, my dear! What happened?"

Lungwort lifted sad eyes. Without a word, he continued

on into the house, retreating into his boot study and drawing the curtain behind him. For a moment Sweet Cicely stared after her husband. Then she dashed into the boot after him.

Only then did the others notice Poppy. She had been standing alone, quite ignored. Now they surrounded her and pelted her with questions. "What's happened?" "Is something the matter?" "What's with Lungwort?" "What did Mr. Ocax say?"

Poppy, not sure how to reply, remained silent. Finally she held up a paw, her father's gesture. The mice responded as they always did. They grew quiet.

Swallowing hard, Poppy said, "Mr. Ocax refused permission for anyone to move."

Like air escaping from a balloon, there was a collective gasp from the crowd. But a torrent of questions followed. "What did Mr. Ocax say?" "Didn't Lungwort explain?" "What are we supposed to do now?" "Did the owl give any *reasons?*"

Poppy lifted a paw again. Once the crowd had stilled, she confessed softly, "Mr. Ocax said it was because Ragweed and I didn't ask permission to go to Bannock Hill."

She hoped for a chorus—or at least one mouse—who would say, "That's not fair!" or "That's absurd!" No such word was spoken.

Alarmed, Poppy looked around. Some eyes avoided hers. Others showed sorrow. Quite a few darted angry glares at her.

"You'll have to excuse me now," she murmured, quite shaken. "I need to get myself dry."

A narrow passage was made for her to pass. As she entered the house, she felt a nudge from behind. Alarmed, she jumped. It was Basil.

"This way," he whispered.

He led her to an isolated room. "Dry yourself," he said. "I'll get you something hot."

Placing Ragweed's earring to one side, Poppy began licking her fur dry. By the time she was done, Basil returned with an acorn of steaming mashed rye. Despite her upset, Poppy ate ravenously, grateful for the warmth that seeped through her body.

Basil listened intently as Poppy told of the meeting with Mr. Ocax.

"And look what I found." She held up Ragweed's earring.

Basil took it carefully. "Where was it?"

"Sticking out of one of Mr. Ocax's pellets."

"Makes me sick," he muttered. After a while he asked, "Poppy, what's going to happen next?"

Poppy sighed. "I thought it would have been impossible to feel worse than I did when Ragweed died. I was wrong. *This* is worse. So many will suffer. And guess who's being blamed? Me!"

Wearily, Poppy made her way to the attic. She wanted to be alone.

Amid Farmer Lamout's clutter she'd come across a tin

can a while ago shaped like a house. "Log Cabin Syrup," the label read. After cleaning the inside to a shiny newness and lining it with her favorite old magazine bits, Poppy considered it her own room.

Now she patted down a wad of filmy lace—her pillow— and crept beneath a blanket—a crocheted doily. Curled up into a tight ball, she tucked in her paws and wrapped her tail about her, tucking its tip right below her nose. Never had she felt so worn out.

Even so, she could not sleep. She kept hearing Mr. Ocax say that he was refusing permission for family members to move because they—she and Ragweed—had not *asked* him if they could go to Bannock Hill.

Then, too, there was his hint that he would change his mind if she sacrificed herself. She was glad she had not mentioned that to the family, rather suspecting some of them would have urged her to do it. The mere hint of such a thing gave Poppy the horrors. She drew herself into a tighter ball.

Harder to deal with was her own inner voice. It kept insisting that if what she and Ragweed had done was the reason for keeping others from moving and being safe, maybe she *should* sacrifice herself. A tear trickled down her face, rolled to the end of a whisker, and dropped into her pillow.

Oh, she thought, if only Ragweed were here. He would have had *something* to say.

But what? she asked, trying to cheer herself up. Most likely a question, a backward one just like the time he asked

Lungwort how Mr. Ocax could confuse huge porcupines with small deer mice.

Even as she thought about Ragweed's asking, Poppy realized that her father never did give an answer. She wondered why.

Poppy forced herself back to her problem. Mr. Ocax said he was refusing permission because of something she and Ragweed had done. How would Ragweed have turned that around?

Poppy could almost hear it: Ragweed would have said, "What did refusing permission allow Mr. Ocax to do?"

Just asking herself the question—because it lifted some of the burden from her—gave Poppy a touch of encouragement. Well, then: *What did refusing permission allow Mr. Ocax to do?*

Poppy tried to remember exactly what occurred when her father finally came to his point and requested permission for the move.

Slowly but clearly it came back: *When Lungwort asked the question, Mr. Ocax became flustered.* He seemed unsure about something, something connected with New House. That is, he didn't ask Lungwort about the *move*, he asked if he had been to *New House*. In fact, he actually asked the question twice. Or was it three times? The point was, the moment Lungwort said he had *not* been to New House, that was when Mr. Ocax said no.

But it was not, Poppy recalled, "No, you can't move." Rather, it was "No, you cannot move to *New House*."

Well, then, what did refusing permission allow Mr.

Ocax to do? *It allowed him to keep the mice away from New House!*

Poppy sat up. Was it possible that there was something there—*at New House*—that Mr. Ocax wanted to keep hidden from them? Was *that* the real reason for his refusal?

The idea so excited Poppy that she felt like rushing downstairs to tell Lungwort. She started to get up—only to stop.

If she had hit upon the real reason for Mr. Ocax's refusal, there was but one way she could prove it. She would have to go to New House and see what was there. And she could hardly ask Mr. Ocax permission to do that!

"I don't care," Poppy said aloud, making a fist of a paw. "I'll do it. I will."

With a sigh of exhaustion, Poppy finally fell asleep. But it was not a restful sleep. She kept dreaming she was lost. Worse, no matter where she turned for help, she saw only eyes—Mr. Ocax's eyes. They were always just above and behind her.

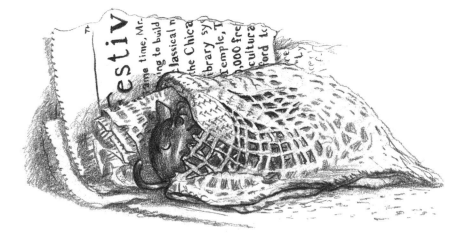

8
Poppy and Papa

From the moment Lungwort pulled the curtain across the entrance to his boot study, he did not show himself. When inquiries were made, the curtain was opened by Sweet Cicely, but merely a fraction. Looking out just long enough to say, "He's not well," she would draw the curtain closed.

Now Poppy stood before the study, working up the courage to speak to him. She kept asking herself—as she'd already done a hundred times—if she really wanted to go to New House. The answer, plain and simple, was *no*. Just the thought frightened her. But still, she was convinced it was the only way to prove that she and Ragweed were not really the cause of Mr. Ocax's refusal. Nonetheless, she feared that when she told her father about her intentions, he would be displeased.

With a sigh she braced herself and called, "Papa!"

Her mother peeked out from behind the curtain. "He's not—oh, Poppy, it's you."

"Mama," Poppy said, "can I speak to Papa, please?"

"Well, if anyone . . . Just make it brief."

Poppy slipped into the boot. "Is he still ill?" she whispered.

Sweet Cicely nodded. "I've never seen him looking so poorly. He lies there whimpering, though every once in a while he'll shake his head and sob, 'What are we going to do?' or 'It's all over with us now.' "

Poppy's heart sank.

"Poppy," Sweet Cicely continued, "I do hope you're going to tell him something that will cheer him up."

"I'm not sure I will," Poppy confessed.

Her mother sniffed. "Well, then, you'd best know what else he keeps saying."

"Oh?"

"He says, 'If only Ragweed and Poppy had asked permission!' "

Poppy's heart sank even further.

"And I must agree with him," Sweet Cicely went on. "Well, if you insist on seeing him, come along."

Lungwort had curled himself into the absolute toe of the boot, the gloomiest part. His tail was wrapped around his feet, his whiskers were limp, and his front paws were in constant motion as if squeezing a sponge. Poppy thought his fur had grown grayer, too.

Sweet Cicely leaned over him. "Lungwort, dearest. It's Poppy come to visit."

Lungwort shook his head, and mumbled as if holding an argument with himself.

Poppy came forward. "Papa . . . ," she said.

Lungwort looked up and stared fixedly at his daughter. "Doomed," he said mournfully.

"Who is?"

"The whole family."

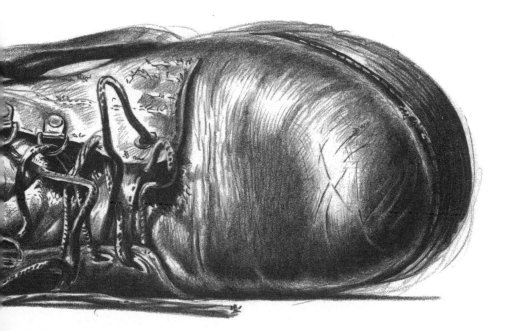

"But . . ."

"If rules aren't followed," he began, but stopped to shake his head. "No, it's my fault."

"What do you mean?"

"If I had raised you properly, you would never have gone to Bannock Hill without asking permission and none of this would have happened. I accept full responsibility." His tail swished in dismay and he started squeezing his paws again.

Poppy appealed to Sweet Cicely with a look, but her mother was gazing piteously at Lungwort.

"Papa," Poppy said, "I have an idea that there may be another reason why Mr. Ocax refused us."

Lungwort sniffed. "You're too young to have ideas."

Poppy didn't protest but pressed on. "I think Mr. Ocax refused permission because of something about New House, something he doesn't want us to know."

Lungwort considered his daughter for a moment. Suddenly his whiskers stiffened and he bared his front teeth. "That Ragweed," he snarled with anger, "he twisted your mind. He's the cause of all this!"

Poppy stepped back as though struck. But she managed to say, "I'm going to try to find out."

"How?"

"I'll go to New House."

Lungwort turned limp again. "Why tell me?" he said with a shrug. "You don't care what I think. You'll go anyway."

Poppy wanted to say something kindly, but the words would not come. Instead, after a painful silence, she turned to go.

Suddenly Lungwort cried, "Poppy!"

"Yes, Papa."

"Look out for porcupines!"

*P*OPPY lay upon the floor of her Log Cabin Syrup room and studied a map of the area. As far as she could see, there were three ways to reach New House. The easiest would be to go along the Tar Road. But if she took that route, she'd be traveling in the open. That was reason enough to rule the Tar Road out. The longest way would be to go around the Marsh, but that meant going over Bannock Hill, and it held too many painful memories—and fears— connected to Ragweed's death. No, Poppy was not ready to go there again. Not yet.

Her third choice was Dimwood Forest. Few mice who had ventured in had returned to tell of their experiences. Even so, the dark woods seemed to offer real advantages. She could travel midday even in bright sun. Mr. Ocax and most other creatures would be asleep then. And if and when the need arose, the same light would enable her to find a hiding place. If the forest had anything, Poppy assumed, it would have plenty of places to hide. She would go that way.

Poppy told only Basil about her plans. If she succeeded in discovering the real reason for Mr. Ocax's refusal, there would be time enough to let everybody know. On the other hand, if she discovered nothing, who would know—or care—if she disappeared?

She asked Basil to meet her at the back steps of Gray House when the sun was at its highest the next day. That morning she mingled with the family so none would suspect what she was up to. But with so many convinced that she was the cause of the crisis, the hostility made it too painful to wait. Some time before her appointment with Basil, she was pacing by the back steps, ready to go.

"I'm leaving right away," Poppy announced as soon as her cousin appeared.

"You forgot something," he said.

"What?"

"This." Basil held out Ragweed's earring. "For courage," he said.

Poppy held still while her cousin gently affixed the earring. When she shook her head, it tickled her ear. "I need a nuzzle," she said, caught in a swell of emotion.

As they nuzzled, Basil whispered, "I could go with you."

Poppy broke away. "It has to be just me," she said, and leaped off the back steps.

"Why?"

"If I'm the one who caused this mess," she called, "it has to be me who sorts it out."

"Good luck!" Basil cried after her.

Poppy, not wanting to look back because she thought it might make her lose heart, dashed away.

9
On Her Way

O nce past the rusty water pump, Poppy had to cross Old Orchard. Mr. Ocax's permission was not required here. Even better, the grass was high among the old twisted apple trees, providing good camouflage. Here and there delicate pink lady's slippers bloomed. Berry bushes were heavy with fruit. Bluebirds, jays, and warblers flitted by. Grasshoppers leaped about joyfully.

"Oh my, oh my," Poppy murmured as she rested halfway across. "It's too nice a day to be worried and sad." She was sitting beneath the shade of a snowberry bush, nibbling on a succulent dandelion stem. Above, only a few high-flying clouds floated in the blue sky.

The graceful drift of clouds reminded Poppy of her secret desire, something she had never told anyone, not even Ragweed. She suspected he would have teased her.

Once, when up in the Gray House attic, chewing through some old magazines, she had come upon pictures of the old ballroom dancing team of Ginger Rogers and Fred Astaire. Here the couple dipped. There they soared. Here they spun. Poppy was enraptured. From that moment on, her greatest desire was to be a ballroom dancer. Oh, to glide effortlessly across the floor in the arms of a handsome mouse!

Forgetting everything for a moment, Poppy plucked a pair of lady's slippers and fitted them to her feet. How cool, how soft and delicate they were, as if someone were kissing her toes.

She jumped up, lifted her arms, flexed her paws—elegantly, she hoped—leaned her head back, fluttered her eyes, and twirled about just as in the pictures. Round and round she spun.

Suddenly—as if a voice actually whispered into her ear—Poppy recalled something Sweet Cicely had told her many times, that "the only live mouse is an alert mouse."

Feeling alarmed—and embarrassed—Poppy promptly

kicked off the lady's slippers, scampered beneath the protection of some stinkweed, and scanned the skies. Yes, she must keep on guard even though Mr. Ocax was probably sound asleep.

Mr. Ocax was not asleep. He was flying over the Marsh in the direction of Bannock Hill. Though working daylight hours displeased him, he was convinced it was necessary. Ever since Lungwort had requested permission to move some of the mouse family to New House, Mr. Ocax had been uneasy. He kept wondering about the mice. Had they discovered what he had discovered? Did they know something he did not? He knew the reason they gave for moving to New House, but were they telling the truth?

Then there was Lungwort's daughter Poppy, who had escaped him twice. The effrontery. How had she done it? the owl kept asking himself. Did she possess special skills? Why had Lungwort brought her to that meeting? Was it to mock him? Was she going to take over from the old fool?

And why did this business of New House and the matter of Poppy occur at the same time? Was it just a coincidence? Could there be a connection? A conspiracy! The more questions he asked, the more nervous the owl became.

Whatever the truth, Mr. Ocax decided that he had to remain on the alert. Sleep less. Patrol more. As his mother used to tell him, "An alert owl is a well-fed owl." In particular, he must keep his eyes open for that mouse, the one named Poppy.

SCAMPERING from bush to bush, Poppy soon reached the banks of Glitter Creek. There she stopped to gaze nervously at the far side and the towering trees of Dimwood Forest. Her first task, however, was to get over the water.

At the spot where she stood, Glitter Creek was as wide as the length of Gray House. Usually the water flowed with tranquillity. Not now. Though the bright water was moving far less rapidly than on the night of the storm, the flow still tumbled, twisted, and foamed around the many rocks that stuck up from the creek bed. Poppy realized that she'd never be able to swim across.

She could walk downstream and cross the Bridge. But the Bridge was situated exactly where Mr. Ocax had his watching tree, the last spot she desired to revisit.

No, as Poppy saw it, the only way for her to get across the creek was by jumping from rock to rock. She climbed a tree stump for a better view, and set about figuring a route. Though it took a while, she found a path that required fourteen jumps. The only problem would come on the ninth. On that rock a turtle was sleeping. Even so, she thought she'd have room enough to make a quick landing and leap away. The turtle might not even notice.

On the creek bank again, Poppy crouched, ready to take her first jump. Just as she was about to spring, she stopped. Once over the water, how could she return home?

Even as she hesitated, a breeze fluttered Ragweed's earring. The tickle it brought reminded Poppy of the reasons for her mission. Resolved anew, she gave a leap and landed deftly on the first of the rocks, then the second, and the third. On she jumped, gaining confidence as she progressed. The eighth jump, however, required a pause. Her next leap would land her on the turtle's rock, but because he had shifted position, there was no longer any room for her to land.

"Hey, Turtle!" Poppy shouted. "Would you please move?"

The turtle slept on.

In search of an alternate route, Poppy noted a small, low rock not far upstream. It was covered with moss. To reach it would require a difficult though not impossible jump. She saw no other choice.

Poppy took a deep breath and kicked. Her leap was high and far enough. She landed right on the small rock, but unfortunately its moss was wet and slimy. The moment she hit it, her feet shot out from under her. A quick skid plopped her into and under the water.

Spitting and coughing, Poppy clawed her way back to the surface. For an instant she floated downstream; then a wave picked her up and pinned her against another rock. "Help! Help!" she cried. The next moment, another wave whisked her away.

M<small>R.</small> O<small>CAX,</small> gliding over Farmer Lamout's fields, heard Poppy's call for help. From the west, wasn't it? He banked sharply and headed in the direction of Glitter Creek.

P<small>ADDLING</small> furiously, Poppy struggled to keep her nose above water. Despite her efforts, she was swept on. She spun downstream like a whirligig. Then, abruptly, she felt herself wedged between two rocks. Water washed over her. As she gasped for air, she sensed that if she stayed put it would be only a matter of time—a short time—before she drowned.

Wrenching one paw free, she groped for something to cling to. What she found was the slimy root of a water lily. She tried to hold on. The root slipped from her grasp.

She reached out again and managed to find the lily's stem. Snorting to keep nose and mouth free of water, Poppy hauled in. Bit by bit she began to rise.

S<small>OMETHING</small> in the water of Glitter Creek caught Mr. Ocax's eyes. To his surprise, he saw a mouse struggling with a water lily.

(71)

POPPY worked frantically to pull herself higher. She was now only belly-deep. With a few more pulls on the stem she would be safe.

CIRCLING above, Mr. Ocax watched the mouse struggle to climb atop the rock. The moment it reached it, he was prepared to dive.

POPPY nearly had her footing on the rock when the lily stem snapped. Her balance lost, she tumbled back into the creek. The moment she struck the water, a wave pummeled her below the surface.

JUST AS Mr. Ocax dived, the mouse he was watching suddenly dropped into the water. When it failed to reappear, he assumed the creature had drowned. His patience frazzled, he pumped his wings, rose on a gust of air, and turned toward New House. A day had passed since he had been there. He needed to check it again.

POPPY, desperate for air, bobbed to the surface like a cork. Once again she was swept along. Her strength was ebbing. Desperately she sought something to hold on to. She found nothing. Down the creek she went.

Then the creek widened. The water grew less turbulent. Aware that this was probably the last chance she'd have to save herself, Poppy summoned her remaining strength and began to swim frantically. Slowly, painfully, she pulled free

of the stream's main force. She bumped against a stone,
then ricocheted into a calm backwater. She stretched her
toes down—and touched bottom!

Half-crawling, half-swimming, she clawed her way up
the creek bank. When she reached the grass, she flung
herself down, coughing violently.

For a long time Poppy lay on her back, eyes closed,
capable of only gasping breaths. Then she rolled over and
threw up the last of the swallowed water. At last she gave
a shuddering groan of relief.

On the northern edge of Dimwood Forest, Mr. Ocax found a branch that allowed him to observe New House without being seen. From his perch he looked past a dirt road, an old barn, a cornfield, a salt lick, and a lawn. What he sought was something else, something he last saw on the new barn next to the house. When he saw it again, he gasped. It was still there. It must be living there. Whatever hopes he had, evaporated.

Poppy opened her eyes. Though her vision was bleary, she was able to gaze up at the sky through the petals of a daisy. She was quite certain it was the most beautiful flower she had ever seen.

Anxious to know where she'd landed, she sat up and looked about. Only then did she realize she'd come ashore near the Bridge. And on the far side of the creek. Feeling pleased with herself, she considered the nearby trees with pleasure.

The next second, Poppy's pleasure vanished. She'd come ashore at the one spot in the whole world she least wanted to be, right next to Mr. Ocax's charred oak.

10
Dimwood Forest

Poppy searched desperately for a place to hide. Glitter Creek ran behind. Before her stood Dimwood Forest. There was little choice. She plunged among the shadowy tree trunks and began running wildly, her only desire to put as much distance between herself and Mr. Ocax's tree as possible.

It did not take long before an exhausted Poppy had to stop. Her sides ached. She was hot and cold all at once. Her heart felt as though it would break out through her ribs. Gasping for breath, she crept beneath a leaf, then peered about to see where she had come.

It was as if the sun had been stolen. Only thin ribbons of light seeped down through the green and milky air, air syrupy with the scent of pine, huckleberry, and juniper. From the rolling, emerald-carpeted earth, fingers of lacy ferns curled up, above which the massive fir and pine trees stood, pillar-like, to support an invisible sky. Hovering

over everything was a silence as deep as the trees were tall.

Poppy gazed at it in awe. She was not sure what she'd thought Dimwood Forest would be like. She knew only that she'd never imagined it so vast, so dense, so dark. The sight made her feel immensely isolated and small. Feeling small made her a part of all she saw. Being part of it made her feel immense. It was so terribly confusing.

The silence was broken by the sound of sharp tapping. Poppy ducked. But nothing happened. From another direction came a yelp. A screech. Poppy shivered. Closer still was the smothered scurry of something slithery and unseen. A tree groaned. A branch snapped. There was the passing scamper of little feet. Poppy's heart raced just as fast.

She could only guess what animals were making such sounds. Automatically she thought of porcupines, recalling vividly the frightening picture her father had shown the family. Had not Mr. Ocax given a special warning about a particularly bloodthirsty porcupine he'd seen recently in the forest? He had. Poppy grew even more tense. She had to find a place to regain her composure.

Anxiously she gazed about for a safe place to rest. What she found was a massive boulder, its top half matted with dark moss, its lower part embedded in earth. Beneath it was a hollow.

Poppy bounded over to the rock. Close up, the hollow proved to be more like a cave, utterly dark at the deep end. What was there? She edged forward, sniffing the air. She froze. A distinct animal smell alarmed all her senses. Unable to identify what it might be, she listened intently, ears flicking this way and that. Seeing and hearing nothing, she crept slowly forward until she was completely inside the cave. Was anything there? Only when she was quite certain nothing was did she begin to clean herself.

MR. OCAX, from a hiding place on the far side of Dimwood Forest, watched the barn at New House intently. His nervous talons clenched and unclenched the branch upon which he was perched. At first he tried to deny the fear he felt inside him. But it was growing too fast. It could not be denied. That he, Ocax, the great horned owl, should feel *fear* made him livid. It was for others to be fearful, not him. "It's unfair," he hissed. "Unnatural!"

Suddenly, hearing his own outburst, he looked about in alarm, anxious that some other creature might see and hear him. No matter what, his fearfulness must never be known! He spread his wings and glided silently away from New House.

In a temper he recalled the mouse he had seen in Glitter Creek. Perhaps the body had been tossed up on the bank. He was upset enough to eat anything, even if it was already dead.

When he reached the creek, he began to fly upstream, moving low over the water.

POPPY paused in her fur cleaning now and again to gaze out at the forest. It should not have been called Dimwood, she told herself, but Darkwood. She kept asking herself how she had ever thought she'd find her way through such a fearsome place. The likelihood of her survival was growing slimmer moment by moment. And though at the moment she felt relatively safe, she worried that she had not gotten far enough away from Mr. Ocax's watching tree. But which way should she go? She had no idea where she was. She was lost and knew it.

She recalled the vow she'd made on Bannock Hill never to leave home again. She considered going back. She wanted to. But then she thought about what would happen if she did return with nothing to report to Lungwort about Mr. Ocax. Life would be miserable.

Poppy sighed. It was so hard to be courageous. So hard to be a coward. Going forward or back seemed equally awful. So much easier to do nothing. But if she did nothing, she would surely perish. What was she to do?

Trying to stay calm, she reminded herself that by pressing on, she at least had a chance to make a difference for her family. Now, if only she knew which direction would lead her to New House.

MR. OCAX concluded that the mouse he had seen in the water was gone, washed away. At least, there was no evidence of its existence—dead or alive. In any case, he was still so upset by what he had seen at New House that he found it hard to concentrate on searching. His head ached. All he could think about was getting some sleep. He would go home.

He flew deep into Dimwood Forest, moving in a northerly direction.

Poppy peered nervously out from beneath the boulder. "If this is midday," she said to herself, "I'd hate to be in the forest at night."

She considered staying and sleeping for a while. But the distinct smell of the other animal made her too nervous. It certainly seemed not to be about. But what if it came back while she slept? Too risky. If she wanted to sleep— and she did—she'd have to find a better place.

Checking in all directions, paying particular attention to the angle of the slanting rays of sunlight, and knowing that moss grew on the north side of trees, Poppy made up her mind that she could make a rough determination as to which way east was, the direction from which she had come.

As she recalled the lay of the land, New House was to the north. She would go north, then, hoping for the best.

Mr. Ocax came to rest on the gray, lifeless tree—a snag—that was his nest. With its top broken off, the snag rose twice as high as a blackberry bush from the ground. A high hole served as an entrance to its hollowness.

For a while the owl sat at the edge of his nest and stared moodily before him, thinking only about what he had seen at New House. Just to think about it made him tense. He felt he was in grave danger. The question was, What kind

of danger? Was he about to lose his food? Would he have to fight? If he did, he knew he might be defeated. If he was defeated, would he have to move to another territory? Was there anything he could do about the situation? It was all so painful to contemplate!

Fretful, the owl scanned his neighborhood, paying special attention to a very large hollow log on the ground not far from his snag. Its ancient thick bark was rust-colored and encrusted with yellow fungus that looked like stubby angel wings. A clutch of pale mushrooms grew from the rotting soil around it. Just the thought of the creature who had recently come to live in the log made Mr. Ocax angry. It was as if the whole world were ganging up on him.

Too tired to think about that now, Mr. Ocax dropped down into his nest. Feeling safe there, he did not take long to fall into a restless sleep.

*P*OPPY made her way northward through the forest in short runs. She could only hope she'd chosen the right direction. Sometimes she paused to eat, but she felt too insecure to stop for long. Her toes ached with tension.

An hour later, Poppy stopped to nibble on some pine seeds. As she ate, she noticed a huge log partly embedded in the earth. Covered with yellow fungus, it seemed very old. And it appeared to be hollow.

Poppy considered it. If the log was unoccupied, it might be the perfect place for her to rest with safety.

Then she noticed the remains of a large gray tree. Its top was gone and it had a hole in its side. It might be safer

than the log. But after studying it, Poppy decided the hole was too high for her to climb to. The log would be better.

Wary, she crept forward. The closer she came to the log, the stronger grew a scent unfamiliar to her. She sensed trouble. She was still sniffing when she heard the sound of a twig snapping behind her. She spun about and gasped.

A red fox, long bushy tail swishing back and forth, was trotting in her direction, its sharp nose to the ground. Poppy understood immediately. The fox was following her scent.

Turning back, Poppy took a flying leap that landed her right at the log's open end. The fox, hearing and then seeing her, barked sharply and closed in, its lips drawn back from its sharp teeth.

Poppy stood trembling before the log. Every instinct in her body warned her not to enter. When she looked back, however, the fox was almost upon her. There was no time to waste. She dived into the log.

The fox stuck its nose in after her, its barking booming about Poppy like a cannonade. Trying to get away, she moved deeper into the musky dark. Suddenly she stopped. At the far end of the log she heard the distinct sound of heavy breathing. It was exactly what she had feared: Another creature was already in the log.

Hastily she turned toward the log opening. She never reached it. The fox's lolling red tongue and sharp white teeth barricaded the way.

Poppy stared back into the log's darkness. The breathing and rattling were drawing nearer. She was trapped.

Erethizon Dorsatum

n the obscure murk of the log's interior, Poppy crouched tensely. Slouching slowly out of the dark came a flat-faced beast with a blunt black snout and fierce grizzled whiskers. Its eyes were heavily lidded as though it had just awakened. The creature moved ponderously, with a waddle and rattle. Its stench was powerful enough to make Poppy clamp a paw over her nose.

The moment the animal caught sight of her, it came to a clumsy stop and blinked. "What the bee's butt are you doing here, fur ball?" it snarled.

Poppy, wishing she knew what kind of animal she was facing, could only whisper, "It's just me, sir."

"The name is Ereth," the animal snapped. "Erethizon Dorsatum. But I just get called Ereth. What's more, I'm a grump and you just woke me up, so don't try to slick me down with slug slop."

"I'm truly sorry I woke you, Mr. Ereth," Poppy said.

"What are those things on your head," the beast growled, "flat balloons or ears? The name is *Ereth*. E-R-E-T-H! And stop your barking."

"Please . . . Ereth, it's not me barking."

"Then who the frog flip is making that racket?"

"It's a fox at the entrance to the log."

"Some idiot friend of yours?"

"Oh no, sir. Not my friend."

"Who the dung beetle bit are you, anyway?" Ereth suddenly demanded. "You're so small I can hardly see you."

"I'm a deer mouse. A girl deer mouse."

"I didn't ask *what* you are. I don't give bug's bathwater about that. I asked for your *name*."

"Poppy."

"Poppy? What kind of idiotic name is that?"

"Please, it's a family tradition. We're named after flowers and fruits."

"Erethizon Dorsatum is my name. Latin name. But you kids don't learn Latin anymore, do you?"

"I don't know what Latin is, sir, I mean, Ereth."

The beast sniffed loudly. "The whole forest is full of idiots. Like that fox."

During this conversation the fox had continued to bark and whine, occasionally even digging furiously at the log entrance.

"Pop, fop, snop," Ereth cried, "or whatever your idiot name is, would you tell that fox to shut up!"

"It's *Poppy*. And if I tell him, I don't think he will."

"Why not?"

"He wants to eat me," Poppy said faintly.

"*Eat* you?"

"Yes."

"Jerk," Ereth said scornfully. "But then all meat eaters are jerks. Ever notice that? I mean, did you ever meet a meat eater who wasn't loud and aggressive? Did you? Never mind, just get out of here and leave me alone."

"I *can't*," Poppy cried.

"Why the bat bilge can't you?"

"I just told you," Poppy pleaded. "If I go out, he'll eat me."

"Look here," Ereth cried, "whatever your idiot name is—don't you have any guts?"

"Please, it's *Poppy*."

"Oh, weasel wonk, I don't *care* what it is. All I'm saying is, if a creature can't take care of himself, he has no business sneaking into my house, waking an old coot like me in the middle of the day, and asking for my help."

"I never asked you for your help," an exasperated Poppy replied. "Can't you understand anything? That fox *chased* me. Do you think I like being in here? It stinks!"

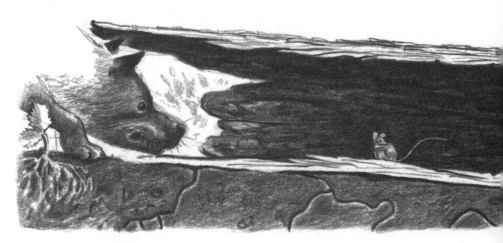

Ereth blinked. "Oh, all right," he growled. "I suppose I better talk some sense into that meat mauler. Just get out of my way!" he snarled as he began to waddle forward. "It's your lookout, not mine, if you get pricked by one of my quills."

Poppy's heart clutched. "Did . . . did you say . . . *quills?*" she stammered.

"Of course I said quills, fuzzball!"

"Yes . . . but . . ."

"But *what?*"

Poppy was dizzy with fear. Her knees shook. She found it hard to swallow. "What *are* you?"

"Don't you have eyes?" Ereth screeched. "Or are those spots on your face buttons? I'm a *porcupine!*"

Porcupine! The word turned Poppy numb. She could hardly breathe. She could not think.

"Floppy or Ploppy," Ereth bellowed, "will you get your flea-flicking self out of my way!"

Poppy dived against the pulpy wall of the log and squeezed herself flat to allow Ereth room. Even so, as the

porcupine waddled by, his quills raked across her belly like a rusty comb. Never—despite all she'd confronted—had Poppy been so terrified.

Ereth, however, continued to make his ponderous way toward the log's entrance, where the fox was still barking and yelping.

Poppy felt sure that once the fox was disposed of, the prickly monster would turn on her. First he would shoot her with his quills. Next he would stab her. Then he would skewer her. Finally he would chop her into tiny bits and eat her!

For a moment Poppy considered offering herself to the fox. If the choice was between being swallowed in one gulp or being tortured by this porcupine, surely death by fox would be preferable.

Poppy stared into the darkness of the log. Perhaps there was an escape hole. But, frozen by the terror of her predicament, she could not move. Instead, her eyes turned toward the entrance, certain she was about to witness some ghastly carnage.

Sure enough, when Ereth reached the log opening, Poppy heard him screech, "Fox, you braying bag of bones, what's all this hullabaloo? Can't an old creature get some quiet in his own home?"

"I'm sorry, Ereth," Fox returned in a voice that was, at best, sniveling. "I didn't know *you* were here. Just trying to grab a mouse who ran into your place. A snack. Nothing more. Not trying to bother *you*. No harm meant. Just a midday nibble."

"Don't nag me about your nibbles, you nitwit," Ereth bellowed. "When I say get lost, I mean do it!"

"Now, Ereth, let's be—"

Fox did not finish the sentence. Instead, Poppy heard Ereth cry, "I said, Get, broom tail!" This order was followed by a *whack*, a yelp of pain, and a frantic scramble of paws, concluding with a barking and whining that grew faint with amazing rapidity.

Poppy was sure the fox was being devoured. But more frightening still, she saw the porcupine wheel about and start to waddle back down the log in her direction. Poppy panicked. She turned and fled toward her one hope of escape, the log's other end.

The farther into the log Poppy went, the more foul-smelling it became. Worse, she had increasing difficulty seeing where she was going. Sure enough, she slammed into the log's far end. There was no escape hole.

Stunned and unsteady on her feet, heart beating so hard she was sure it would burst, a terrified Poppy turned to confront the porcupine. Her one remaining hope was to try and slip by the beast. Though Poppy knew she risked a severe shredding, she was certain it was her only chance.

"Slop, Pop, or Bebop," the porcupine cried, "where the snake sweat are you? Come out of there!"

Gasping for breath, Poppy braced herself against the rear wall of the log and got ready to bolt and die.

Ereth's face, grinning hideously, loomed out of the dark at her. "Poppy," he cried, "you wretched excuse for a runt, why the devil are you hiding in my toilet?"

12
What Poppy Learns

on't stab me!" Poppy cried through chattering teeth. "Don't kill me!"

Ereth blinked. "What?" he said.

Poppy staggered forward, fell to her knees, held up her paws, and bowed her head. "Don't eat me!" she implored.

"What the lice lips are you talking about?" Ereth asked with genuine bewilderment.

Poppy gazed up tearfully. "If you're going to kill me, do it quickly. Just don't torture me, *please!*"

"Why would I want to torture you?"

"Because that's what porcupines do when you catch mice. You torture them and eat them."

"Eat *mice!*" Ereth exclaimed. "Hit the puke switch and duck! Meat disgusts me. Nauseates me. Revolts me. I'm a vegetarian, jerk. I eat bark."

"Bark?"

"You saying I'm a liar?" the porcupine roared.

"Well, no, except—"

"Except nothing. I'm kind. I'm gentle. I'm old. All I want is to be left alone."

"You won't eat me?"

"*I don't eat meat!*" Ereth bellowed into Poppy's face.

Poppy gulped. She was beginning to feel very foolish. "Well," she offered lamely, "everybody thinks you do."

"Well, then everybody eats grasshopper gas."

"They do?"

"How many times do I have to tell you," Ereth screamed. "I DON'T EAT MEAT!"

"But—but," Poppy stammered, "didn't you just eat that fox?"

"Are you crazy or something? All I did was swat him with my tail, which is what I do when creatures get fresh with me."

"What about shooting your quills?" Poppy asked. "Or—or stabbing with them?"

"Where'd you hear this bat bilge?"

"I—I was taught."

"Poppy—that's your name, right?—quills are *hair*. Barbed hair. I can't shoot my quills, though they fall out easy enough. The only way a quill gets into you is because I slap you. Which I'll do if you mess with me. Mind, when a quill gets into you, it swells. Flex your muscles to get it out, and the barbs draw it in deeper. Hurts like the red-hots. Want to see for yourself?"

"No, please! Please! I believe you," Poppy cried. "I just didn't know that. Really. I'm sorry."

"Probably isn't your fault," Ereth grumbled in a somewhat softer tone. "I suppose you get taught that garbage in school."

"We go to school at home," Poppy explained. "Lectures. And tests."

"Who's the world-class idiot who told you that porcupines eat mice?"

Poppy was about to say her parents when she suddenly realized something she hadn't thought of before. She began to speak, but, fearful of saying the name, she held back.

"Well," demanded Ereth. "Who?"

Poppy leaned forward. "Mr. Ocax," she whispered.

"Ocax!" Ereth yelped. "The great horned owl? *Him?*"

Poppy nodded. "He told my parents and they told us."

"Ocax . . . ," Ereth said, and he began to laugh.

"What's so funny?" demanded Poppy.

"Let me get this straight," Ereth said. "Ocax told your folks that porcupines eat *mice?*"

"Well, see, Mr. Ocax protects us from porcupines. What's so funny about *that?*"

"Poppy," Ereth said between fits of sputtering laughter, "*he's* the one who eats mice! And if there's one thing that jerk of an owl is frightened of, it's *me.*"

"*You?*" Poppy cried with astonishment.

"Listen, Poppy, nobody messes with Erethizon Dorsatum. *Nobody.* Fool with me and I'll shove a quill up your snooter. The only thing that old owl wants is to protect himself. Why, he wouldn't get within a log's length of me. I may be old and fat, have a foul mouth, and smell, but I can shake my tail and put it in his face! Yours, too. Want to see?"

"No," Poppy replied quickly. "I believe you, Ereth. Really I do."

"Protects you from porcupines . . . ," Ereth said with a sneer. "Frog flip! But if you believed that, what the worm water are you doing here?"

"I was trying to get to New House," Poppy explained. "And honest, that fox did chase me."

Ereth snorted. "But you said Ocax told you to be scared of me, is that right?"

Poppy nodded.

"Poppy," Ereth said, "running in here was smart."

"It was?"

"Sure. The truth is, you could walk by the side of a lake, with no place to hide, if I were there. That jerk of an owl would do no more than look at you."

"Really?" Poppy said, feeling a great sense of relief.

"If there's one thing I like beside being fat, sassy, and prickly to the touch, it's going where no one wants me to go. Fact is, I'm one of the few creatures in Dimwood who can protect you. I bet that's the reason he says all that earwig juice about me.

"As for New House, don't talk to me about going. Just go. I never tell anyone what I do."

"Don't you have any family?"

"Oh, I had parents. And a wife. For a while there we even had kids. Quite a nice bunch. They all wandered off. We all go our own ways. Prickly."

"Don't you miss them?" Poppy asked.

"I like being alone. If I see a tree I want to climb, I climb it, chew some bark, then get some sleep."

"Isn't there anything in the world you love, really love?"

At the word *love*, the look on Ereth's face turned dreamy. He sighed. "Yes," he admitted. "There is."

"Who is it?"

"Not who, Poppy. *Salt.* I can't get enough of it. I'm mad for it. I'd die for it. It's because of my liver, someone told me. I don't care. I love it. Rock salt. Sea salt. Sweat salt. Any kind of salt." He licked his lips. "Don't happen to have any on you, do you?"

"I'm sorry, I don't."

"You were talking about New House. You have any idea what's there?"

"That's what I need to find out."

"I'll tell you one thing that's there."

"What?"

"A chunk of salt as big as me. Humans put it out for deer. Can you believe it, *deer!* But it's on a high steel pole, so I can't get it. What a waste. Oh, but I do dream about it. I do." He closed his eyes.

"I think Ragweed would have liked you," Poppy said with admiration. But even as she spoke, a great wave of exhaustion swept over her. "Please, Ereth, would you mind very much if I took a nap?"

"Poppy, you can do what you want. But if I were you, I wouldn't sleep where you're standing. As I told you, it's my toilet, and it's too stinky even for me."

13
Early Morning

Within the log, but not too far from its entrance, Poppy found herself a soft place to sleep. There, curled up in a tight ball with her tail tip parked right below her nose, she felt safe enough to sleep. When she awoke after a long, sound slumber, it was dark and quiet. She got up slowly and stretched her aching muscles, then looked about for some sign of Ereth. The old porcupine was nowhere to be seen. Was he gone for good? Not likely, Poppy knew, but he might be gone for hours.

She also knew she was hungry. Cautiously she made her way to the log's opening. It was night, and she could see neither sky nor stars. A silver sheen of moonlight made lace of the canopy of trees above even while transforming the ground into a carpet of velvet gray. She sniffed the air. Mingled with the sharp scent of pine and fir, she breathed

in delicious hints of good things to eat: nuts, berries, seeds, fragrant flowers, tender roots.

There were sounds, too: the creak and groan of trees, the sudden, shrill cries of animals, the occasional fuzz-buzz of passing bugs.

Poppy could only feel astonishment. This was not Dimwood the forbidding. This was Dimwood the beautiful, a luxuriant world that teemed with life, a universe that held more than she had ever seen or dreamed of, a paradise that filled her with an almost aching desire to dance through it and see more.

Trembling with excitement, Poppy was about to take a step away from the log when she chanced to look up. On the gray, lifeless tree with a hole on its side, an acorn toss from where she was, perched a brooding owl.

The moment she saw the owl, Poppy darted back into the safety of the log. There she stayed, her heart thudding. Had the owl seen her? She did not think so. Could it, in fact, be Mr. Ocax? If it was, how could he have tracked her? But perhaps it was another owl. She had to know.

In any case, her elation was gone. The forest was not to be for her. She sighed at the fright she felt.

Poppy tried to calm herself. First she pondered over her discovery that Mr. Ocax had lied about porcupines. At least she did not have to be frightened about them. In spite of herself, she giggled when she thought about Ereth. Such a likable unlikable creature.

Then she thought of what else Ereth had told her, that Mr. Ocax was actually afraid of porcupines. The notion that the owl was afraid of anything gave Poppy considerable pleasure. Perhaps he was afraid of other things as well.

So Poppy thought again about her suspicion that there was something at New House that alarmed the owl. Oh, if only there was. If only she could find it.

Feeling more hopeful, Poppy returned to the log's

threshold to wait for Ereth. She wanted to take another look at the owl but was afraid to. Instead she sat, content for the moment to gaze out at the beautiful forest.

*T*HE OWL Poppy had seen was indeed Mr. Ocax. He was perched upon the entrance to his home, flexing his sharp talons and staring gloomily into the forest. Now and again he swiveled his head and blinked, then clacked his beak. Hungry, he wished that something—anything— would reveal itself by moving.

Once, just out of the corner of his eye, he thought something moved at the entrance to the old log that lay not far from his snag. But it was gone so fast he could not be sure.

Was it the porcupine? He hoped not. He hated Ereth. Just the thought of him made Mr. Ocax drop down inside his snag. Better to sit in the darkness and listen than deal with that creature. If something came by, he would hear it.

"*W*HEN are you leaving for New House?" Ereth asked Poppy. The old porcupine had made his way back to the hollow tree before sunup. Bits of bark were stuck about his lips, chin, and whiskers.

"Soon," Poppy replied evasively.

"Good," Ereth said. "You're a sweet kid, but I like my privacy."

"Ereth," Poppy began after a moment, "I know you

want me to go, and I want to go, too, but when I looked out before, I think I saw an owl."

"On that snag just beyond my door?" asked Ereth.

"The *what*?"

"The old tree with a broken top."

Poppy nodded. "There was an owl sitting there," she said. "I was told Mr. Ocax lives in Dimwood. Could . . . could that be him?"

Ereth snorted. "Follow me." Somewhat anxiously Poppy trailed the porcupine out of the log. "That the snag you're talking about?" Ereth said, pointing.

"Yes."

"Well, then, that's where Ocax lives."

Poppy jumped back. *"There?"*

"Absolutely."

"Don't you mind?" Poppy whispered, edging closer to Ereth.

"Naw. He's a jerk. Anyway, he doesn't get near me."

"But he rules this whole territory."

"Him? Rule? Maggot milk."

"But . . . but it's true."

"Poppy," Ereth snorted, "there are lots of creatures who live around here. Some are mean, like Ocax. Some are sweet, like me. Nobody rules."

"But he says he does."

"Oh, bee's burp. Just because you're scared of someone doesn't mean you have to believe him." Ereth turned toward the snag. "Ocax!" he bellowed. "Ocax!"

"No," Poppy cried, "don't!"

It was too late. Mr. Ocax popped up in his snag hole. In a panic, Poppy scrambled to hide behind Ereth's tail.

"What do you want?" Mr. Ocax demanded.

"I've got a mouse here by the name of Poppy who says you've been calling yourself ruler of Dimwood. That true?"

Instead of answering, Mr. Ocax shifted his head, trying to catch a glimpse of Poppy. When he saw her timidly peeking from behind Ereth's tail, he jutted his head forward, opened his eyes wide, and hissed.

Ereth laughed. "She also told me you claimed porcupines eat mice. That you protect them from me. Ocax, do you believe that garbage, or do you just like the way it tastes in your mouth when you say it?"

Suddenly Mr. Ocax's eyes narrowed. "Where did you get that earring, girl?" he shrieked at Poppy. "That something I ate?"

Poppy became so frightened she began to back up.

"What I eat is mine, girl, mine!" Mr. Ocax screamed.

"Listen here, Ocax," Ereth snapped. "This mouse has as much right as you do to go and do what she wants! I don't want you messing with her!"

But Mr. Ocax, ignoring Ereth, only cried, "Poppy, listen to me! I don't know what you're doing here, but you might as well know the only way you'll ever get back to Gray House is when I dump your dead carcass on your father's front porch!" With that he clacked his beak, then dropped down inside the tree.

Alarmed and furious, Poppy ran forward and began beating her clenched paws on Ereth's nose. "You lummox!" she cried. "You lump! You rattling pincushion!"

The porcupine only grinned.

"Why did you tell him about me!" Poppy shouted. "Didn't you hear what he said? He's going to kill me!"

"Oh, he's nothing but fuss and feathers. He doesn't bother me."

"But you've got quills," Poppy protested.

"Jealousy don't become you, girl."

"Ereth," Poppy implored, "I have to get to New House. It's a matter of keeping my family alive."

"You're pretty small to be a heroine."

Poppy looked down at her toes. "That's not the only reason I'm going."

"Oh?"

"It's also because of Ragweed."

"Who?"

"Ragweed. He was . . . my friend." Poppy sniffed. "See,

he wanted to ask me to marry him atop Bannock Hill. Said it was the most romantic spot around.

"I did want to marry him, so I said I'd go, but only after asking permission of Mr. Ocax. That's the rule. But Ragweed said, 'Where's the romance when you have to ask permission?'

"So we went without asking. When Ragweed and I got to the top, he did ask me to marry him, but before I could answer, Mr. Ocax killed him.

"Then, later, the owl said it was because Ragweed and I went to the hill without permission that my family couldn't move to New House. When they heard that, a lot of them—most of them—blamed me."

Poppy pushed the tears away. "So you see, I'm going to New House to prove our being on the hill had nothing to do with Mr. Ocax's refusal. If I don't prove it, my family can't go to New House and we'll be ruined. I'll be ruined! So I have to go. Only now that you've told Mr. Ocax I'm here, he'll follow me and keep me from finding the truth. You've got to come with me."

Ereth shook his head. "Sorry, kid, this is your business, not mine. Anyway, I need to get some sleep." Yawning, Ereth turned and began to move toward the log.

"Ereth," Poppy cried out, "if you got me to New House, I'd—I'd get that salt for you."

Ereth stopped short and spun about. A dreamy look filled his eyes. "The salt lick? From New House? The *whole* thing? You would? Really?"

Poppy placed a paw over her heart. "I swear."

Ereth grinned. "Now you're talking, girl. Let's move it!" Without a moment's hesitation he began to lumber through the woods.

Poppy took one look at the snag in the dawn light, then tore after the porcupine.

THE TWO of them had barely gone when Mr. Ocax popped out of his hole. Having heard the entire conversation, he wasn't sure which he felt more, fury or fear. But he did know he had to stop Poppy. He launched himself into the air.

14
On the Way to New House

The old porcupine moved faster than Poppy thought possible, body swaying from side to side, quills rattling like a snare drum.

The trail Ereth took was narrow but smooth, avoiding hills, tangles, and fallen trees. From time to time Poppy saw other animals: weasels, a raccoon, a ferret, and, once, a bear. As soon as they caught sight of Ereth, they hurried away in haste.

Poppy bounded along after Ereth, pausing now and again to gaze upon the endlessly enticing forest with delight and amazement. In low places, white ground mist eddied gently, while above, in the high trees, the early sun sowed golden sparks among dark leaves. But once, while Poppy was staring wide-eyed at a particularly towering tree, she caught sight of what appeared to be a brown blur swooping among the pines. Her joy melted.

"I think Mr. Ocax is following," she called to Ereth.

Ereth, however, did no more than grunt and press forward.

Poppy caught up with him and from then on stayed as close as possible. But with every third step she glanced back. Finally she actually saw Mr. Ocax. He was high above, gliding through the treetops on widespread wings like a silent phantom.

"He is following!" Poppy cried.

"Bug brain," Ereth mumbled.

Then, no matter how much Poppy searched—her neck grew strained from so much turning and twisting—she lost sight of the owl. At last she decided he had gone. More relaxed, she paused now and again to take in the forest views.

It was while she stopped to sniff a Scotch broom plant that Mr. Ocax, out of nowhere, made a dive at her, talons flashing.

"Ocax!" Ereth bellowed. Without looking, Poppy leaped toward Ereth for protection.

The porcupine, for all his bulk, whipped about and lifted his tail, prepared to strike with his quills. Mr. Ocax pulled up short and, hissing venomously, flew aloft and vanished.

"That was close," Poppy panted. She was trying to see where Mr. Ocax had gone. "What made you notice him?"

"Poppy, if you think there's anything that's going to keep me from that salt, you don't know me." Once more the porcupine trundled along the trail.

"Ereth," Poppy panted, straining to keep up, "I'm certain Mr. Ocax wants to keep me from New House. There *must* be something he doesn't want me to see."

Ereth stopped abruptly and gave a snort. "Poppy, some creatures aren't worth trying to figure out. If they bother you, what I say is, swat 'em with your tail."

"Ereth, not every tail has quills."

"You're right. I shouldn't hold yours against you." He set off again.

"Ereth," Poppy said after a while, "if I could just find out what it is that Mr. Ocax is frightened of and tell my family, I wouldn't care what happened to me."

Ereth laughed sarcastically. "Even if it kills you?"

"Well, no, but—"

"Poppy, if you don't stay alive, the only thing you'll be good for is maggot mash."

As they traveled farther, Poppy noticed that the trees were growing less dense. There were greater varieties of flowers, too. As the brightness intensified, Poppy guessed that they were reaching the northern limits of the forest.

"Ereth," she said, "when we get out of the woods, where will we be?"

"First there's a dirt road and an old barn. Then a field of corn. Beyond the field is some low grass, then the buildings where the people live. There's also a new big barn. That's for chickens."

"What are people like?" Poppy asked. Other than pictures in the magazines back home, she had never actually seen any humans.

"They don't bother me."

"Do they dance a lot?"

"What's dancing?"

"It's gliding, swirling, dipping, and sliding with someone you like."

"You are strange," the porcupine said. "Now, don't try to distract me. On the short grass—not far from the cornfield—is the salt lick. You figured a way to get it for me yet?"

"Ereth, I haven't even seen it," Poppy answered.

"It's beautiful, Poppy," Ereth murmured, "really beautiful."

They had reached the northern edge of Dimwood Forest. Beyond the last of the trees, Poppy saw a dirt road. Even farther was a dilapidated barn—smaller than Gray House and considerably older. It stood on the edge of the field, leaning over slightly. The field itself was full of tall stalks bearing plump and tasseled ears of corn. Tossed by a gentle breeze, row upon row rustled and whispered with heavy ripeness.

Ereth trotted across the dirt road.

"Come on, move it," the porcupine scolded once he looked back and saw Poppy on the other side.

"I'm checking for Mr. Ocax," Poppy called across, though since the owl's one attempt to grab her she had not seen him. Deciding he was either gone or hiding, she darted across the dirt road and rejoined Ereth.

"Let's go!" the porcupine cried, and plunged into the cornfield, beating his way through the stiff stalks. Poppy paused now and again in his wake to snack on fallen corn, which lay about in great quantity.

Compared with the fallow fields the mice scoured near Gray House, the profusion of food here was a marvel. Back home, the food the family had access to took long hours to find, and there wasn't that much of it. Here was food enough to feed a family twice their size. Was it this rich field that Mr. Ocax wished to hide? Did he want her family to go hungry? All that searching for food out in the open did make them more vulnerable.

"There!" Ereth cried, when they finally burst through the far side of the cornfield. "Look!"

Poppy sat up. Before her was a neatly cropped grass lawn. Not far from them stood a smooth shiny pole as high as a cornstalk. It was capped by a large block of white salt.

"Isn't that *something*," Ereth whispered. Poppy glanced at her friend. He was drooling.

Now that Poppy could see what she had promised to bring Ereth, her heart sank. How in the world would she be able to do it? It was perfectly clear that even if she could manage to get the salt off the pole, it was too huge for her to carry.

The problem itself was too huge to carry. With a sigh, Poppy looked farther. Beyond the salt lick was a white house. It bore some resemblance to Gray House, but its paint was bright and its windows were newly curtained—

signs that suggested that people were living there. Was this what Mr. Ocax didn't want them to know about?

Poppy turned to the left and saw a red barn. It was considerably larger than the house but had only a few windows. The roof was highly pitched and covered with sheet metal. At the front end of the barn the roof jutted out to form a door hood. Poppy gasped. Sitting right below the overhang near a large, closed window was an owl—an owl twice the size of Mr. Ocax.

15
Alone Again

Ereth moaned softly. "Isn't that the most luscious thing in the whole world?" he asked, gazing at the salt lick.

Poppy, whose eyes were fixed on the enormous owl, could hardly speak. "It's awful," she barely squeaked.

Ereth turned to her. "What are you saying?" he demanded.

"Look!" cried Poppy, trembling, as she pointed to the owl on the barn.

Ereth turned, looked. "Never noticed that before," he grunted.

In wonder, Poppy murmured, "Mr. Ocax is only half that size."

Ereth shrugged, then went back to gazing at the salt. "Well, girl," he said, "have you figured out how you're going to get that salt for me?"

Poppy, still in a state of shock, managed only to shake her head.

Ereth took one last, loving look at the salt and turned. "You know where to find me," he said. "Don't let me down." With that, he began to waddle away.

"Ereth!" Poppy cried, her fearful trance broken. "Wait!"

The porcupine peered around peevishly. "What now?" he grumbled.

"You aren't just leaving me here, are you?"

"What else am I supposed to do?"

"Help me," Poppy said in a small voice.

"Poppy, we made a deal. I'd get you here. You'd get me that salt. I've done my part. Now you do yours."

"But—"

"No buts," Ereth snapped, lashing his tail in irritation. Poppy backed away. "I'm going home now, but I'll be waiting." With a final glare, he said, "Keep your promise, fur ball," and marched off.

Poppy started to run after him but tripped on something and fell flat. When she got up, Ereth had disappeared among the corn.

An unhappy Poppy dusted herself off. It was then that she noted what had tripped her. It was one of Ereth's tail quills. When he'd flounced his tail, it had fallen out.

Poppy picked the quill up gingerly. She'd never really looked at one closely before. It was mostly black and made of long, fused hairs, just as Ereth had said. One end was blunt. The other end, the sharp end, was ivory-white. With fascination, Poppy examined the tiny barbs. The point, which she was unable to resist touching, was frightfully sharp.

She was about to toss the quill away when she had an idea. Grasping it by its blunt end, she swished it about a few times. It moved nicely. Like a sword.

Poppy found a tall blade of grass, plucked it, and tied it around her waist in sash-like fashion. With care, she slid the quill under this belt. It fit comfortably. Then she drew the quill out a few times to see if it came free easily. Though a single quill was not the full arsenal that Ereth carried, it was something. She only hoped she'd never have to use it.

Reluctantly, Poppy turned her attention back to the enormous owl on the barn. The bird had not moved but was still sitting on its perch, gazing off into the distance with huge eyes. Poppy was relieved it had not turned her way.

The realization that at any moment the owl might turn and discover her made Poppy retreat into the corn, but not so far that she'd be unable to peer out. Once hidden, she tried to make sense of her situation.

It was all very well to have reached New House. But now that she'd arrived, she still had no real clue to why Mr. Ocax would not permit them to move here. All she had seen was this huge owl. Could his reason have something to do with that?

Poppy tried to think it through. An owl of this size would be ferocious. Perhaps Mr. Ocax was worried that this bird would steal his food. It certainly would eat a lot.

The truth was—and Poppy forced herself to acknowledge it—this huge owl made moving here impossible. Mr. Ocax was bad enough. This owl looked twice as bad!

Then Poppy had a new thought: Was Mr. Ocax really trying to protect her family? Had she been wrong about him all along?

But then, perhaps this owl was not really living here at New House? Simply because she was seeing it now proved nothing. It could be passing through, perhaps just spending the night.

The sun was up now. Poppy decided she had best settle in, and wait to see what—if anything—happened.

16
The Truth at Last

I t was some time before she sensed movement in the house. It appeared as vague forms stirring behind second-floor lace curtains, then shifted to the windows below. The front door opened. A tomcat poked his head out. He looked around, stepped outside. The door shut behind him.

He was a large, bony orange cat, with the pinched body of advanced age. One ear was bent. He walked slowly, limping slightly, glancing up at the sun as if to measure its warmth. But by keeping his tail high, he maintained a stately dignity.

Poppy held her breath. Surely the huge owl would notice the cat and realize the old beast had little fight in him and less speed. It would be no trouble at all for the owl to snatch him up.

Nonetheless, the cat continued to saunter casually toward the barn. He stopped once, then twice, to scratch himself stiffly under his chin. When he reached the barn, he sat directly below the owl. Squinting, he looked into the sun, then lay down and closed his eyes. Through all of this the owl did nothing.

It made no sense. But Poppy kept watching. The cat slept. The owl remained motionless. The field of corn rustled.

Once again the house door opened. This time a human emerged, a boy. In his hand he held a long stick with a string and a small hook attached to it. Momentarily, he stood on the threshold of the door, apparently listening to something being said from within. He nodded, and shut the door. Then he started off on the same path the cat had taken, toward the barn.

Poppy, who had never seen a real person, watched with fascination. Surely, she thought, the owl would fly away the instant it saw this human coming. Big as the owl was, the boy was much bigger.

But though the boy drew nearer and nearer, the owl remained motionless, its open eyes fixed on something distant.

The boy reached the cat, bent over, and patted it. The cat flipped his tail, but continued to sleep. Then the boy looked up at the owl. He showed not the slightest surprise to see it there. Instead, he put down his stick and went inside the barn.

With the barn door open, a few chickens strutted out,

clucking and pecking the ground.
They paid no mind to the cat *or* the
owl. Nor did the owl consider them.

Poppy was completely baffled.
What could the owl be looking at that
so held its attention?

The next moment she was even more startled to see
the upper barn window open—the window right next to
where the owl was roosting. It was the boy who opened it.
Even so the owl did not budge. More amazing, the boy
reached out, placed his hand on the owl, and turned it
about so that it now faced in a new direction!

Never had Poppy been more astonished. Could it be
that this huge owl was not real? *Was it only a fake?* It
certainly seemed so, but after all, she had made but one
observation. What she needed was proof. To get it, she
would have to wait at New House and watch.

Poppy stayed on the edge of the cornfield. But her time
was not all spent waiting. She was too excited to remain
in one place. Instead, she took time to explore the old
barn at the other edge of the field—by the dirt road
—and found it a respectable addition to
Gray House. As for food, Poppy had never
eaten so well. It was as she had first
believed: There was enough in
this cornfield to feed her family.
In fact, all of them
could move here.

During her hours of watching, Poppy met with no other small animals. At first she was perplexed. Then she decided it was because the fake owl was successful. It had frightened everybody away.

Not that Poppy put aside her porcupine-quill sword. She remained sufficiently wary to keep the sword at her side.

Once she almost used it.

At midday she was trying to take a needed nap when she suddenly heard something coming through the corn behind her. Taken by surprise, she leaped up, darted behind a cornstalk, and drew the quill, ready to defend herself.

It was a family of deer, a doe and two young fawns, though to Poppy even the little ones seemed enormously tall. Even so, they had not the slightest interest in her. Instead the animals threaded their way through the corn and approached the salt lick cautiously. With the mother standing guard, the fawns took a few delicate licks of salt until, at a silent signal, they all bounded away.

As Poppy tucked the quill back under her sash, it occurred to her that she might enlist the deer's help in bringing the salt to Ereth. But from the way they had enjoyed themselves it did not seem likely that they would be willing to take the salt to the porcupine. No, she would have to find another way to make good her promise. Besides, the questions about the barn owl were more pressing. As far as Poppy could tell, it had yet to move on its own. Though Poppy was fairly sure it was a fake, she had to be positive.

That afternoon Poppy thought of a way of getting proof. The old cat was still stretched out where he had begun the day. The more Poppy observed the cat, the more certain she was that he was too old to be dangerous. She decided to ask him about the owl. The notion made her a little nervous, but she convinced herself that keeping her quill sword at the ready would be enough protection.

With considerable care, she crept out of the cornfield, all the while eyeing the barn owl—just in case. It did not move. At last she was standing before the sleeping cat, close enough to feel the wash and smell of his fish-scented breath. He was snoring. Gripping her quill tightly, but using her friendliest voice, Poppy shouted, "Hello!"

The cat opened one eye.

"Hi there," Poppy said.

"Howdy," the cat murmured. Although he had now opened both eyes, he did not move.

"My name is Poppy."

The cat sneezed delicately.

"Bless you," Poppy said.

"Thanks," returned the cat. "They call me George."

Poppy nodded. "Nice place you have, George."

"Pleasant enough," George replied.

"Ah . . . well . . . that owl sure keeps things quiet around here," Poppy offered.

"Owl?"

"The one up on the barn."

"Oh, right. The fake one," said George. "Does the job," he said.

"What job?" Poppy asked carefully while trying to contain her mounting excitement.

"Keeps everybody away. Even other owls."

"How do you know?"

" 'Bout two weeks ago the people here put in some chickens. First day some big old horned owl snatched himself one. Next day the people put up that fake owl. About two days later—I was watching—that real owl came back for another chicken. I saw him dive. Saw him catch sight of that fake owl."

"What happened?" Poppy asked. Then she held her breath.

"That owl put on his air brakes so fast he flipped right over himself. Must have been scared silly," the cat said with a mostly toothless grin. "Funniest thing I've ever seen. And I'll tell you, that was the last time I've seen that owl around here." The cat closed his eyes. "Mighty funny," he murmured.

Poppy could hardly keep from grinning. "Nice talking to you, George," she said.

"Have a nice day." The old cat sighed and resumed his snoring.

Poppy all but skipped back to the cornfield. Despite her

excitement in proving the barn owl was fake, she made herself settle down and think things through carefully.

The owl was fake, but Mr. Ocax believed it was real. Afraid of an image of himself, he was probably fearful that he would no longer be the one to rule over the mice. *But*—according to Ereth—Mr. Ocax was not really a ruler. That was a lie, just as it was a lie that he was protecting the mice from porcupines, whom he actually feared himself. In fact, the owl was full of fears!

Suddenly a whole new idea burst upon Poppy. *Was it possible that Mr. Ocax's claim that he was protecting mice was merely his way of getting to eat them?* The notion was astounding. But the more Poppy thought about it, the more it seemed to be so. It certainly explained things. That is,

Mr. Ocax's refusal to give permission for the mice to move to New House had nothing to do with what she and Ragweed had done. He had refused because he did not want the mice to know how fearful *he* was of losing his dinners!

But if that was true, then the mice could come to New House whether Mr. Ocax liked it or not. It was not for Mr. Ocax to decide where they lived but for the mice themselves! And oh, irony, if the family moved to New House, the fake owl would protect them.

Poppy was so sure she had found the truth that she stood up on her hind legs, leaped into the air, and kicked her heels twice. When she landed, she collapsed into a soft heap and allowed herself a great sigh of contentment. With that, she closed her eyes, and fell into a deep sleep. What a day!

As POPPY slept, Mr. Ocax flew in to settle on a branch along the edge of Dimwood. From deep within the foliage he stared furiously at the owl on the barn.

17
A Surprising Conversation

oppy woke refreshed. For a moment she just lay still, luxuriating in her discoveries. She imagined telling her family what a phony Mr. Ocax was. What a delicious moment. Yes, it was time to return home.

Realizing that she was very hungry, Poppy first treated herself to a big meal, eating only the plumpest corn kernels. Hadn't she deserved them?

Gradually she ate her way over to the dirt road that ran alongside Dimwood Forest. With her mouth full and her belly tight, she gazed across at the wall of pine and fir. She had feared it before. Now, knowing it, she recalled only its dark beauty, its deep fascination.

The forest made her think of Ereth and her promise. How was she going to get him the salt? She still had no idea. Then and there she vowed that once she got home, she would return, maybe this time with cousin Basil. Perhaps the two of them could find a way.

Poppy thought about Mr. Ocax, too. Wouldn't it be fun to tell him what she had discovered? The image of it made her grin. The liar! The bully! It was while she was thinking about him that she spied him.

Mr. Ocax was perched deep within the foliage on a small tree right by the edge of the forest. If it had not been for the slanting rays of the sun, Poppy might never have noticed. It was the light of his glowing eyes that caught her attention.

Poppy crept forward. When she came near the row of corn closest to the forest, she looked up again.

A moody Mr. Ocax was staring at the barn across the field. He kept moving his head about, back, forward, side to side, hissing and clacking his beak. Sometimes his black talons kneaded the branch with nervous tension. At other times he ruffled his feathers, lifted his wings, let his head sink lower. Poppy could tell he was miserable, sulking.

She had to marvel at how different he appeared from the time she'd seen him on his watching tree in the rain. All that glaring and hissing. He's just a frightened bully! she said to herself with jubilation. She had to slap a paw over her mouth to keep from laughing out loud. What fun it would be to humiliate him. Just the idea of it brought a feeling of power.

Unable to resist teasing him, she called out, "Mr. Ocax!"

The owl, taken by surprise, looked up, down, around.

"Here!" Poppy cried. "In the corn. It's me, Poppy."

Mr. Ocax hunched over and peered in her general direction. "Show yourself," he said harshly.

"I'll stay where I am, thank you," Poppy returned. Wedged in as she was among the cornstalks, she felt totally secure. She knew he could not reach her there.

"Mr. Ocax," she called, "is it the owl on that barn you're looking at?"

"What's it to you?" he growled.

"You're frightened of it, aren't you?" Poppy said.

Mr. Ocax opened his beak, but no sound came out. Instead, he kept peering into the corn.

Poppy said, "It's awful to be frightened, isn't it?"

"What did you say?"

"I said, it's not fun being frightened, is it?"

To this Mr. Ocax said nothing.

"I could tell you a little something about that owl," Poppy called, feeling altogether giddy with her knowledge.

"What is . . . that something?" the owl asked.

"Want to talk about it?" Poppy offered, suppressing a giggle. "Well, I might as well say it to you—I'm going to tell my family."

Mr. Ocax shifted uncomfortably on his perch. "I'll talk," he said. Then he added, "But we could talk more easily if I could see you."

To Poppy's ears, the owl's tone had shifted. It was not nearly so hostile as it had been. Was she only imagining that? Should she trust him? But even as she asked herself that question, she thought, Oh, the look on his face when I tell him that the bird he's so frightened of is nothing but a fake! Aloud, she called, "Would you really like to talk about it with me?"

"Yes, I would," replied Mr. Ocax. "You seem to be a very smart mouse."

Poppy blushed. No one had ever called her smart before. This, she had to admit, was a very different side to Mr. Ocax from what she had known. Ragweed, in his way, had challenged him. As for her father, he had been very timid in his approach. Perhaps the owl would respect someone who stood up to him politely but firmly. "Do you really think I'm smart?" she inquired.

"I certainly do," the owl said. "Yes, perhaps the two of us should just sit down and talk. The two smart ones. Maybe we can work something out."

Poppy felt a stirring of excitement. Here she was, Poppy, talking in a perfectly reasonable way with the great Mr. Ocax. It was she, with her new knowledge, who had gained power. Perhaps, instead of humiliating him, she could work things out reasonably so the mice could move to New House. Wouldn't *that* be a trophy to bring home! So thinking, she moved from her hiding place a little onto the dirt road.

"Yes," Mr. Ocax said soothingly, "let the two of us talk things over. I should think we could find some reasonable solutions."

"All right," said Poppy. Boldly she stepped farther out on the road. She looked up. Mr. Ocax was gone. "Where are you?" she cried. At that moment the owl plunged down upon her from behind.

18
The Battle

Ragweed's earring saved her. So powerful, so swift was Mr. Ocax's descent that he pushed a wave of air before him and caused the earring to flutter. The flutter felt like the tap of a tiny finger on Poppy's ear. She felt it and whirled. At the last possible second she saw the owl coming and made a leap to safety.

The next moment, however, she realized she had made a terrible mistake. She had leaped, not back among the corn, but farther onto the open road.

Mr. Ocax was now on the ground, blocking her way to the field. She spun toward the forest. In a second the owl was up in the air and down on the other side. Once again he had blocked her way.

"Not so smart as all that, are you?" he sneered. "Well, I don't compromise with what I want," he told her. "And what I want is you never getting home alive." He made a sudden darting movement to the left. Poppy jumped to the right, but Mr. Ocax was ahead of her. Just as quickly he shifted back toward her, so that Poppy was forced to halt herself clumsily. There she stood, flat-footed, panting, not sure which way to go.

The owl, towering over her, laughed. "I told you what would happen if I caught up with you again, didn't I? But this time you won't have that fat porcupine to help you." So saying, he made a snap at her with his beak.

Mr. Ocax's mention of Ereth was the reminder Poppy needed. She reached down and yanked the quill from her sash, then held it before her like a sword.

At first Mr. Ocax blinked. Then he snickered. "You don't think *one* of his quills is going to stop me, do you?"

"That owl on the barn," Poppy panted between hard breathing, "is just a fake! You've been frightened by a fake owl!"

Mr. Ocax's beak dropped open. He hesitated. In that moment Poppy sensed she could have gotten away. But she could not resist another taunt. "You're not an owl, you're a chicken!" she cried in triumph.

For an instant the two of them, owl and mouse, confronted each other. Then a look of terrible rage passed across the owl's face. Poppy knew then she'd made another blunder. She'd lost her momentary chance of escape. Now there was nothing he'd not do to kill her. She would have to fight him.

Trembling, she flourished the quill. In response, Mr. Ocax spread his wings, then beat down hard with them upon the road. They threw up a cloud of dust.

It was hard for Poppy to breathe, much less see. She took a step back, only to hear a sound behind her. Confused, she turned. Hidden by the dust, Mr. Ocax had overleaped the road. Once again he was behind her. From there he made a slash at her with his beak. Poppy struck out with her quill.

Seeing the quill and realizing the danger to his eyes, the owl pulled back. He glared at Poppy. He snapped his beak.

Poppy stared back grim-faced, gasping for breath, waving the quill before her.

"If it takes the whole night, I'll wear you down," Mr. Ocax hissed. "All it takes is one mistake on your part. Then you're done. Finished." He made a forward feint. Poppy danced nimbly back.

Mr. Ocax struck again. This time it was not with his beak but with his talons.

Poppy, quill up, dodged the talons with a quick side step, but she knew her only hope was to get into the corn and hide. Otherwise, the owl would overpower her.

Making sure of her footing, she began to back toward the forest. Just as she had hoped, Mr. Ocax leaped up and landed between her and the trees. It was then that she raced for the corn.

Mr. Ocax was just as fast. Grasping her strategy, he

barely touched earth when he took a flying hop forward to block her way.

He advanced wildly now, snapping and snarling. In response, Poppy slashed wildly with her quill. Once she struck out at the owl's face but only hit his feathers. But though the blow glanced off harmlessly, it served to infuriate him.

Mr. Ocax, closing in, darted his head in and out, side to side. Poppy was bewildered. Then the owl turned briefly away from her. In a flash, she made a successful rolling dive under his wing. She was behind Mr. Ocax at last, on the corn side of the road. She started to run. He turned his head in a complete half circle, saw her, and spun his whole body about, his right wing extended full length. The wing tip struck Poppy a glancing blow to her head. Down she tumbled and landed on her back in the dust.

Seizing his advantage, Mr. Ocax pounced, beak open, tongue out, hissing. Poppy whipped the air with the quill. The tip of it pricked the owl's tongue. He screamed in rage, and reeled back.

Poppy had just time enough to regain her feet. Once more she faced him, quill at the ready.

Mr. Ocax, stung, pressed forward now this way, now that, head bobbing, weaving, viciously snapping with his beak.

Increasingly exhausted, Poppy was forced to give ground. She crumpled to her knees. It was the moment the owl had been waiting for. With a powerful kick, he thrust his left claw—talons spread wide—at Poppy's head.

Poppy saw the claw coming. Using all of her strength to grip the quill, she held it up with both paws to protect herself, and jabbed it into Mr. Ocax's claw as it came down.

The owl gave a great squawk, fell back, and began to roll about violently. Fearful of losing the quill—her only weapon—Poppy pulled on it with all her might. But the barbs had caught. She could not get the quill loose. She was being dragged and bumped along.

Mr. Ocax, screeching and flapping his wings wildly, flailed into the air. Before Poppy knew what was happening, she, too, was in the air. She did tell herself to let go of the quill, but by the time the thought was whole, it was too late. To drop from the height Mr. Ocax had already reached meant a fall to certain death. There was nothing to do but hang on.

Mr. Ocax, squawking, hissing, flew like one possessed. Up, down, and around he went, making loops and stalling dives, climbing and twisting, anything and everything to work the quill from his claw. But the more he flexed and twisted, the more the barbs worked themselves into his claw, causing ever more excruciating pain. Poppy hung on.

The fact that Mr. Ocax was dragging a claw, and from that claw dangled a mouse, greatly impeded his flying. His flight path became increasingly wild. In his desperate desire to rid himself of pain, Mr. Ocax ceased to look where he was heading.

Violently, he plunged toward the cornfield. Once over it, he lowered his left claw—and that meant Poppy—deliberately thumping it and her along the cornstalks in

the hope that the quill would be jerked out. Poppy was being battered. But each time she decided to release her hold on the quill, the owl surged forward, causing her to cling to it more convulsively than ever.

Knowing she could not take much more, Poppy tried to see ahead. Mr. Ocax was skimming low over the corn tops, but when he passed beyond them, he dropped toward the ground.

Let go! Poppy told herself. Let go! But she was feeling so groggy, her own muscles would not respond.

Then she saw what the owl was aiming for. The salt lick! And he was picking up speed. In his madness he was preparing to strike his claw on that. Poppy had wits enough to sense that if she struck the hard salt, it would be the end for her.

Let go! Let go! she cried to herself again. This time she did. Down she plummeted.

As she did, Mr. Ocax first rose, then dropped. Totally out of control, he slammed into the salt head on. So great was the blow that the salt shattered while the owl went tumbling head over tail in an explosion of feathers. After three flips he ignominiously flopped down like a sack of potatoes onto the ground.

As for Poppy, she had landed on grass. For a moment she lay there, stunned, battered, and confused. She looked up into the sky but saw nothing. Then she looked across the lawn. She saw him then. Mr. Ocax lay on his back, perfectly still. His claws were drawn up over his chest, slightly curled. The quill still stuck out of the left one. Scattered about among the feathers were chunks of salt.

Poppy stumbled to her feet. She took a wobbly step or two toward the cornfield. Then she stopped and looked back. Mr. Ocax had not moved. She stared at him.

Slowly, not sure if she should believe what she was thinking, she crept closer to the fearsome owl. After every few steps she paused, looked, sniffed. Still there was no movement.

Close to Mr. Ocax's head now, Poppy stopped again.

The owl's great eyes were wide open, staring up into the sky. His devil-like tufts of feathers were bent. His beak was open. As Poppy watched, it snapped listlessly.

"Mr. Ocax . . . ?" No answer. She took a step closer. "Mr. Ocax . . . ?"

His head turned slightly. For a moment his eyes seemed to focus on her. "Sometimes . . ." he murmured, "sometimes I . . . wonder . . . why I bother . . . to protect . . . you." With that his beak made a final clack shut. His eyes closed. Poppy knew it then. Mr. Ocax was no longer alive.

19
The Return

For a long time Poppy gazed at the lifeless body of Mr. Ocax. She thought she should be feeling triumphant joy. Plain gladness would have been good enough. Somewhere she did feel pride. But small as she was, it was buried deep. What Poppy felt was weariness, as if she had aged four seasons over the last hour. She felt old.

Before her on the grass lay one of Mr. Ocax's feathers. Poppy had never really looked at an owl's feather. This one was quite lovely. It was a mottled brown color with a white tuft on top, soft as any baby's breath. She picked it up. In the breeze, the vanes stirred slightly.

With a sigh, Poppy slipped the feather into her sash. Then she turned and looked at the cornfield. At first she thought what she most desired was to lie down and sleep. It was growing dark. But a moment's thought made her realize sleep was impossible. What she needed to do was tell someone about her discoveries and what had happened.

She crossed the dirt road and moved along the edge of the forest. There was enough of the porcupine's lingering scent for Poppy to find the trail that Ereth had used to go from his home to the field. For once—and it made her smile wanly—she was grateful for the old fellow's stink.

Plunging directly into Dimwood Forest, Poppy traveled slowly, methodically, taking the time for proper precautions. Now and again she paused to absorb the lush view, the way moonlight filtered through the fragrant air, a very tall tree, a particularly beautiful fern, a bush laden with blackberries as big as her head.

When Poppy reached Ereth's log, she paused long enough to contemplate Mr. Ocax's now abandoned snag. Who, she wondered, would live in it now?

"Ereth!" she called into the log from the entryway. "Are you home? Ereth!"

In response there was some scratching and snorting deep within.

"That you, Ereth?"

"Who the snail squirt is that?" came the growled reply. "Can't a creature have any privacy around here! Beat it unless you want to eat a quill sandwich."

"Ereth, it's me, Poppy."

"Who?"

"Don't you remember? Poppy."

"Poppy!" came the echo, with more enthusiasm than before. A great rattling and shuffling could be heard. Then

Ereth's grizzly flat face loomed out of the darkness. "That really you, girl? Where is it?"

"Where is what?"

"The salt! Didn't you bring it?"

"Ereth, it's about Mr. Ocax, he—"

"I don't give a flea's flick for that jerk of an owl. Where's the salt you promised me?"

"It's there. By New House. All broken up on the ground."

"On the ground!" Ereth shrieked. "What's it doing there?"

"Ereth, I couldn't carry it, and besides—"

"On the ground. Great snail swoggle! It'll melt to nothing!"

The porcupine came barreling by so fast, Poppy had to leap aside. The next moment he was all but running down the trail.

"Can I sleep here?" Poppy called after him.

"Can't stop to talk," Ereth called back. And indeed, he was gone.

Poppy stepped into the log, lay down, and was asleep at once.

She slept until the sun was high. When she woke, Ereth had not yet returned, so she went out, found some seeds, ate them, returned to the log, and slept again—until dusk. This time when she awoke, Ereth was there. He was chewing—in a roisterous, slobbering way—on a chunk of salt.

"Hello," Poppy said.

Ereth didn't even look up. "Delicious. Best salt I ever had." He licked his lips. "Awesome."

"Then you got some of it?"

"Some of it? *All* of it! I'm just about ossified. This is the last bit. It was all pure, wonderful salt. Absolutely delicious. Amazing. Divine."

"Ereth?"

"What's that?"

"Did you see Mr. Ocax?"

"Oh, yeah, him. Dead. What happened?"

Poppy told him. The porcupine, though busy with the salt, slowed his slobbering to listen. When Poppy finished her story, she asked Ereth, "What do you think?"

Ereth shook his head. "Never thought I'd appreciate that owl's hard head. But if what you say is true . . ."

"It is."

"Well, I'm grateful he broke up this salt lick. Really, Poppy, it's incredible stuff. Want some? I mean, a small taste?"

"Ereth . . ."

"What's that?"

"I'm going home now. May I come back and visit?"

"Sure, Poppy, sure! Anytime, and bring some salt."

"I'm going now. . . ."

"Poppy!"

"What?"

"You're the salt of the earth!"

Poppy crossed Glitter Creek by using the Bridge. The

rest of the way she traveled by the side of the Tar Road. By the time she reached Gray House, it was late. The first thing she noticed was that the red flag was flying.

She climbed the porch steps slowly. Instead of going right inside, she took a peek. The entire family was gathered in the front parlor. Lungwort stood atop the old straw hat, apparently in the middle of a speech.

". . . And so, dear friends, we will have to break up the family. Yes, disperse. Go our separate ways. Forage on our own. There is insufficient food for us here. But first I wish to engage in a brief memorial tribute to our full family, which—Poppy? Is that you, Poppy?"

She stepped inside. All the mice turned to stare.

Poppy gazed at them evenly. Then she pulled the feather, Mr. Ocax's feather, from her sash and held it aloft for all to see. "Mr. Ocax is dead," she said solemnly. "And I can tell you that New House is right next to a big field of corn that has enough to feed us all forever and ever."

"Ah, Poppy," Lungwort cried triumphantly, "didn't I say that if you listened to my advice, all would be well!"

20
A New Beginning

Almost thirteen full moons to the night since Mr. Ocax killed Ragweed, Poppy and her husband, Rye (how they met and married is another story), stood on Bannock Hill with their litter of eleven young mice. They had formed a circle around a small hazelnut tree. Looking on, beneath a full golden moon, was Ereth, the porcupine.

"This tree," Poppy was saying to her rather restless children, "was planted, after a fashion, by my late and dear friend Ragweed.

"I can't be sure that it was he who dropped the seed nut from which this tree has grown, but I would like to think so. Though it is rather frail now, someday this tree will be mighty. I want to affix this"—here she held up a small earring—"to a high branch, so as the tree grows, it will glitter in the sky for all of us to see."

"Hey, does Ma love making long speeches, or does she?" whispered one of the litter to one of her brothers.

"And here on Bannock Hill," Poppy went on, "once forbidden to us—though we, too, live in Dimwood Forest— we shall have our dancing place. It doesn't matter how you dance, my children, slow or fast, by jumps or steps. As long as you are free to dance in the open air by the light of the moon, all will be well. Now, Ereth, if you please . . ."

Old Ereth, murmuring "Mouse muck" under his breath, gave a grunt, but began to shake and rattle his quills, until he settled into a steady beat. Then the eleven young litter mice began to dance their own way, with jiggles and jumps, and leaps and lopes. As for Poppy and Rye, they spun round and round in a stately waltz, dancing by the light of the moon and the earring, which glittered high on the hazelnut tree.